The Lion of Farside

Volume 2

John Dalmas

Sky Warrior Book Publishing, LLC

Published by Sky Warrior Book Publishing, LLC.
PO Box 99
Clinton, MT 59825
www.skywarriorbooks.com

Cover Art by Jay Larsen
Cover Layout by M. H. Bonham
Editor: Carol Hightshoe
Publisher: M. H. Bonham

Printed in the United States of America
  0 9 8 7 6 5 4 3 2 1

This book is for
Jerry Simmons and Sarge Gerbode
and for the
Spokane Word Weavers

My thanks to (alphabetically) Eileen Brady, Mary Jane Engh, Jim Glass and David Palter, for their perceptive critiques. And most especially to Hank Davis at Baen Books, for a critique which will prove of lasting value to me as a writer.

PART 4: Strange Alliances

Chapter 25: Embassy

Entering it for the first time, the capital of Tekalos made a drab impression on Liiset, nor did the raw freezing wind of Three-Month help. Teklapori was large, as towns went in the Rude Lands, with main streets less narrow than some, but it lacked aesthetics. In the section they'd just entered, the buildings, built one against another, were two-storied, of wattle daubed with clay, and its whitewash was grimed with dust and soot. Daub repairs formed dirty brownish patches, small and large, unwhitewashed; its thatched roofs were gray from weather and mold. Outlying sections had included buildings made of lumber, bricks, or squared stone, some with tiled or shingled roofs, but wattle and thatch prevailed there too. Regardless, the smell was of slops: human and cooking wastes, primarily. On Farside, she told herself, Evansville's worst slum didn't begin to smell as bad.

She could have bypassed the town and ridden directly to the palace, a mile outside it, but she'd arranged it this way. She wanted people—lots of people—to see them and be impressed.

And she was in charge! Given the purpose of the mission, Idri had at least to seem subordinate, and at any rate wasn't entirely back in Sarkia's good graces. But the two of them worked well together, and had discussed this project thoroughly in advance. For some unknown reason, Idri had always liked her, different though they were. While Idri's abrasiveness, troublesome to many Sisters, seldom bothered Liiset. When it did, she told Idri, and Idri handled it reasonably. Liiset credited their compatibility to some close past-life friendship.

Sad, she thought, that Idri hated Varia so. Varia in a Tiger barracks! What a cruel situation! Hopefully she'd get pregnant soon and be out of there.

The street was lined with spectators, out to see the fabled Sisters. She wouldn't disappoint them. Even her guard section was marvelously outfitted, its tailored uniforms black, its polished, silver helmets and cuirasses blinking in the late winter sunlight. Its horses, individually handsome, were beautifully matched, their coats glossy black, with white blazes and socks.

In the past, the travel costumes worn by Sister diplomats had been elegant but subdued, and typically the Sisters had numbered three. This time...As the Dynast's special envoy, she wore a silver coronet that sparkled with jewels—diamonds and zircons—and her thoroughly brushed red hair was plaited with gold threads. Her riding breeches and tunic were shamrock satin, reinforced with kidskin where practicality required. The cape that protected her from the chill preequinoctial wind was of rich and glossy fur, nearly black: *Martes pennanti*, the pekan, from the Eastern Empire of the ylver. It had reached the Sisterhood via the lords in the mountain, who traded freely with ylvin merchants. Idri's clothing was similar, but her tunic and breeches were glossy blue and her cape merely mink, while the jewels in her coronet were less precious. Each had two attendants of her own clone, similarly dressed but uncrowned, their capes of bulkier, less expensive furs. All six rode matched, red-gold geldings, glossy with good grain and much brushing, these too with nearly identical socks and blazes.

She didn't doubt Sarkia's new foreign policy would work as intended. It had its drawbacks, compared to the old: There were more commitments, not all of them fully compatible. But it would soon rebuild the Sisterhood's status and influence.

Meanwhile they'd enjoy the more agreeable aspects of the mission. She chuckled. *Especially Idri*, she told herself. Idri's role was perfect for her.

* * *

Gurtho had seen Sisters twice before, when his father was king and he'd been a child, once at age six or eight, and again at eleven or twelve. The first pair had seemed to him very beautiful, the other pair merely good looking. Which kind would these be?

We'll soon see, he thought. Six of them! To his casual half-comment, half-question, the evening before, their courier had answered they were "quite beautiful," a generality that only fueled his imagination.

Meanwhile he was edgy. He'd heard about the rape at Ferny Cove, had been excited by it. He'd also heard Sisters described as untouchable, and wondered if he'd dare. Certainly their influence had been reduced, and their army as well.

But what of their magicks? What revenge might they take if he molested one of them? True there were those who said their powers were trivial, but others swore they were deadly. And what the ylver could get away with, and what he could get away with, might be very different.

He knew what his father would say, had heard it more than once: "Never decide with your testicles, boy. That's what brains are for. Base your decisions on the power and money they'll bring. Power and money! Always! With power and money, you can buy whatever you want, including beautiful women. And property, when you're tired of it, can be sold or traded, or given as political gifts. Or killed, if it suits you."

Gurtho had taken the advice to heart. An actual wife was necessary to provide an undisputed heir. Which he now had, along with younger backups, in case the first died or proved unsuitable. But he'd bought his bride, rather than marry politically or in passion. To satisfy his gluttony for women—beyond ladies of the court—there were tax girls. Those he got pregnant he had killed. The others, when he tired of them, he sold, perhaps after loaning them to one of his officers as a sign of the Royal Favor.

* * *

Word of the embassy's arrival was brought by the captain of the envoy's guard, ushered in by Rogell, the palace chief of protocol. The envoy, the captain said, was tired from her ride. At her request, the embassy had been shown to its apartments, where they would bathe and nap and have their hair dressed before supper (which the envoy hoped she and her deputy might eat with His Majesty).

She could have paid her respects first, Gurtho thought. *Well. At supper then.* He ordered Rogell to take word to the steward that supper was to be private—the Dynast's envoy, her deputy, and His Majesty. A formal reception would be scheduled for a later date, with appropriate guests.

* * *

At supper, Gurtho was hard-pressed not to stare. Briefly he was disconcerted that they looked so young, but the envoy's self-possession soon dispelled that. Their beauty was not so easily recovered from, and Idri, he had no doubt, was the most *desirable* woman he'd ever seen. Even her name he found seductive, and spoke it in his mind. Idri!

Still, he ate essentially as he might have. Their small talk went well enough, and neither woman was aloof, nor even reserved. When they'd finished dessert, it was the envoy who brought up business. "The Dynast is interested in establishing a permanent embassy here," she said.

"Indeed?" He wondered if Idri might be named ambassadrix.

"She's never placed a permanent embassy before, except with the King in Silver Mountain. Now she's considering placing several. Yours first perhaps. After all, Tekalos is one of the larger kingdoms, and you are one of the most powerful kings."

"And we love your countryside," Idri put in. "I for one would not object at all to being located here. I can imagine how lovely it will be when the buds burst, and wildflowers line the roadsides."

Gurtho's pulse quickened. "Indeed! We already have flowers in bloom around the palace."

"We saw them," Liiset said, "daffodils and tulips, mostly," then returned the talk to business. "The Dynast is also interested in the possibility of alliance. If you think you may be, we should discuss it."

"Indeed! I might well be interested," Gurtho said. "How long will you remain?"

"A week. The Dynast has one misgiving. She likes her allies strong, and clearly, Gurtho and Tekalos are that, but it's a strength impaired by internal discord. Your Kullvordi hillsmen revolt in almost every generation."

Gurtho frowned. What had that to do with anything? "True," he said, "but we never allow it to become a threat. Just this month, at my orders, the reeves whose shires include the hill districts sent soldiers in and burned the farmsteads of some tax cheats, making examples of their families. Now the hillsmen most inclined to rebellion will rise up, showing us who they are so we can destroy them."

"Ah. And are these Kullvordi good fighters?"

He shrugged. "Not good enough. We always win. Easily."

"What would they be like if you could recruit them for your own army, and train them properly?"

"They'd never join my army. I doubt that as many as a dozen have in my own and my father's time combined. And those who did were lazy and insubordinate."

The envoy nodded. "Of course. If they had no loyalty to their own people, they'd hardly be loyal to someone else."

"Exactly!" said Gurtho, misunderstanding.

It was Idri who spoke next. "You're a strong ruler. We appreciate strong men."

"Yes. Well, one must be, in my position." He turned to the butler and snapped his fingers. "More wine, Elwar," he said. "Whatever best follows the pastries."

Bowing, the butler left the room, and Gurtho returned his attention to the Sisters. "How do two such lovely women pass the time when they aren't doing the duties of envoys?"

"Our duties occupy more of our time than you might think,"

Liiset answered. "For example, before coming here, we read a great deal about your kingdom."

"Indeed? I wasn't aware a great deal had been written about it. I trust it was complimentary. Was I mentioned?"

"Complimentary enough we've looked forward to being here. And yes, you were mentioned in the more recent writings."

"Who writes these things?"

"Travelers. Visitors. Merchants."

"Hmh." Gurtho wasn't sure he was pleased.

"We also play," Idri added.

"Play? At what?"

"Among other things," Liiset said, "Idri plays the lap harp." She turned to Idri. "Would you like to play for the king, my dear?"

Idri looked demurely at Gurtho, then at her hands in her lap, and smiled. "It would gladden me to give pleasure to such a king as Gurtho."

"Well then," Liiset said, and for a long moment seemed to ponder in silence. Gurtho waited. "Have you ever heard our music of spring?" she said at last. "We favor it in this season. Much of it was written for ensembles, but even more for solo instruments. Including the lap harp."

"I'll send for an instrument," Gurtho said.

"She has her own; I've called for it already."

"You have?"

"Through the mind. Many of us can speak through the mind to those we're most closely related to. One of my aides should be here momentarily." Briefly they sat talking; then an outer guard entered.

"Your Majesty! A young woman wishes to give something to her lady," the man said awkwardly. The "young woman" looked so much like the envoy, Gurtho felt sure they were twins. She delivered to Idri a lap harp hardly twenty inches high.

Idri tuned the instrument while the others watched, then began to play, with skill if not inspiration, the music alternating between bright, dark, and serene. Soon, though, Gurtho became restless, and seeing this, Liiset yawned delicately. "Excuse me," she said, "but I haven't entirely recovered from our long ride. I'm afraid I must retire."

"Already, dear Sister?" Idri asked. "His Majesty seems bright-eyed, and as far as I'm concerned, I can play the night away."

Gurtho's pulse quickened. "Indeed," he said, "don't take her away so soon. Let her play some more. I can understand your being tired, and certainly won't be offended if you leave us. But as for me—her playing enchants me more than you might imagine."

"Well…" Liiset looked questioningly at Idri, then seemed to have her answer. "If you wish. Idri and I planned to sleep late tomorrow anyway. Very well, my dear."

Somewhat to the king's surprise, the envoy stood and bowed, rather as a man would, showing cleavage that made the breath stick in his throat. "I wish Your Majesty a most pleasant night," she said, and left.

Alone with the enchanting Idri! He could hardly believe his good fortune. Meanwhile she began to play something sensuous, exotic.

"Are there words to it?" Gurtho asked.

She smiled. "It's a love song, supposedly by an ylvin emperor to his favorite concubine." She began to sing, the lyrics subdued but passionate, suggestive, exciting Gurtho.

"I wish you might play for me alone," he said earnestly when she'd finished.

"But I am."

"I mean, without these." He gestured at his guards.

"Well then, tell them to leave."

He stood, giving his order to their sergeant. In a minute they were gone. "Now that we're alone," Gurtho said, "this room seems too large. There is another, more intimate…" He gestured toward a door near a back corner.

She stood demurely, the small harp under one arm. Gurtho took her other arm, leading her gently, his heart thuttering. The smaller room had a luxurious couch, mirrors with expensive, nearly true surfaces, large pillows distributed here and there, and several upholstered settees. He hoped it wouldn't alarm her; it was the setting for occasional small orgies staged for special friends. Leading her to a settee, he seated her near the middle and sat down beside her, his left knee touching her right.

"Let me sit by you," he said, "and feel your sweet warmth as you play."

"Of course, Your Majesty." She put her fingers on his arm. "If I seem a little breathless…I've never before been alone with a king."

"Ah, and I'm not just any king," he murmured.

"I knew it," she whispered, "when I first laid eyes on you. You are a—king among kings, a—man among men."

He found his hands reaching, his arms slipping round her, his mouth moving to hers. They kissed.

"Oh, Your Majesty," she breathed, and they kissed again; his tongue caressed her lips, and they opened to him. He felt her hand rest on his thigh, and he fumbled at her vest-like girdle. She undid the laces and guided his hand inside it to her left breast, round, firm, hard-nippled. Her own hand slid up his thigh to his cod-piece. For half a minute they fondled one another, kissing, then he could wait no longer, for he was king, and accustomed not to courtship or seduction, but to having, taking. Dropping to his knees before the settee, he began to reach up her skirt, pawing amongst a confusion of petticoats, till she stayed his arm. "Your Highness," she murmured, "it's not necessary to muss my clothing. We need only remove it, mine and yours."

* * *

Gurtho often thought of himself as inexhaustible. It was, his father had told him once, a family trait. But even so…Lying back for the moment, he wondered fleetingly if he'd been bewitched. No, he told himself, this had not been sorcery. Not unless thighs and buttocks, fingers, tongue and lips, were the instruments of magic. *I never imagined a woman like her,* he thought. And had an insight of his own, something rare as summer snow: *It's as if she knows what I'm feeling, and what to do next!* Now that, he told himself, would be most worthwhile magic.

She purred in his ear. "Your Majesty seems tired."

He grunted. "Even a satyr must rest now and then. Briefly. Long enough to let the sweat dry a bit."

Her laughter was low and throaty. "Dry? We needn't wait for that," she said, and swinging astride his thighs, began to lick the sweat from his hairy chest.

Chapter 26: Collecting Taxes

Macurdy turned in the saddle, glancing back at the Big Dipper wheeling inexorably through its nightly course, and remembered that night shift by the watch fires, at the abandoned squatter's farm in Oz. How long ago? Less than three months; it seemed longer. He'd been a runaway slave with just three friends backing him, one of them a bird that might weigh fifteen pounds. Now he was Captain Macurdy, with his own little army: some two hundred seventy rebel fighting men.

He grunted inwardly. *Or would-be fighting men.* Tonight he'd find out how good fifty of the more advanced were; how much they'd learned.

He didn't try to set the pace himself. As a Hero, he'd come to be a skilled rider, but he still lacked a sure feel for how hard and long one could push a good horse. So he'd appointed Tarlok route leader. Just now the man rode in front of him, with a pair of scouts out of sight ahead.

He scanned around, seeing the countryside by the light of a newly risen moon a bit less than half full. Dogs barked from sleeping farms, but farm dogs barked at everything that moved—cats, possums, skunks…No one's sleep would be seriously disturbed unless the tone became excited.

He expected to return a different way; a way with fewer hills to cross, easier for the pack string, which by then would be heavily loaded. And more importantly, a way that would lead their pursuit into Wollerda's ambush, for the purpose of this raid went beyond plunder.

Macurdy had planned the mission as carefully as he could,

given his limitations of time and information, and still felt uncomfortable about it. His Kullvordi officers, on the other hand, were enthused. As he'd explained his thinking to them, they'd reacted as if he was a genius to have thought all those things through.

His basic problem was that he questioned whether his force was ready for something like this. Though he'd gone out of his way not to show it, because one of the pluses was their generally high level of confidence: They had the idea any hillsman was worth three soldiers and six bailiff's men.

Despite his misgivings, here he was, his timing dictated by opportunity and need. To feed his growing company was a constant problem. Also, some sort of successful fighting action was necessary to keep up morale; to keep recruits coming in; and to prevent excessive desertions, because so far, many of his volunteers had shown limited tolerance for training in the absence of fighting. It was also desirable, though not yet urgent, to show Wollerda and his men Macurdy's Company was capable of effective action.

And finally to suggest to the flatlanders the king was in real trouble this time.

The opportunity was the timing of tax collection in the flatlands, and what it might mean to the problem of feeding his rebels. They ate no more as fighting men than they would at home, but at home they ate their own food—food they'd either helped to raise, or bought and paid for. But here…Chits or not, most of the farmers they took food from considered themselves more or less plundered.

Then someone had mentioned the flatlanders were about finished with their wheat harvest, and maybe they ought to raid them.

Macurdy's lips had drawn into a thoughtful pucker. To plunder flatland farmers would kill the hope of rural support there, but he saw another way. He'd already heard how, in the flatlands, the bailiffs' tax squads went out with hired wagons and drovers within a few days after harvest, collecting the tax grain and tax cattle. And presumably as soon as that was done, the farmers would begin carting to market whatever surplus they had, beyond household needs and seed, and no doubt a reserve.

No, he'd announced, *we're not going to plunder the farmers. We'll plunder the bailiffs instead.* Which meant they'd be robbing the king, which would please the farmers (he hoped), and gain the rebels their passive approval at least. While plundering the concentrations in a bailiff's grain bins should be a lot handier than going from farm to farm. And perhaps safer, because they could strike, load up, and get back to the forest far more quickly.

Even his own staff, who were quite willing to plunder flat-land farmers, saw the logic of it.

They'd been ready to do it cold. In fact, their concept of planning in general troubled Macurdy. Their attitude was *no problem. We'll just go do it.* Then he'd point out problems, and they'd say *oh yes,* and listen while he asked questions, paid attention to their answers, and came up with handlings, or what he hoped were handlings.

He had no doubt his Kullvordi were resourceful. The unforeseeable things that would inevitably come up, they'd probably handle better than most would. That was pretty much the way the hillsmen lived life. But the more things you foresaw and prepared for in advance, it seemed to him, the easier it would be to handle the rest of it.

Anyway they'd listened; even been impressed and enthused. Partly because he was going to let them fight at last, but even more because they had confidence in him, in his leadership. More confidence than he did. Not that he denigrated what he'd accomplished, from that decisive morning at the House of Heroes, to the confrontations with Slaney and Orthal. And in building and training his company since then. But to him, the challenges ahead seemed much greater. While to his rebels—he'd performed what they considered miracles, and they assumed he'd continue to.

He looked around at the platoon riding quietly through the night. Only occasionally had he heard a murmured exchange or comment. Beyond that was only the soft plod of hooves on dirt and the squeak of leather; they were doing a good job of keeping route security. He could sense no extreme tension, and he'd come to appreciate how sensitive he'd grown to other people's unexpressed emotions, since Varia and Arbel had worked with him. *These guys are a lot more interested in fighting than Slaney's men were at the fallen timber,* he told himself. *Even with the cover of forest hours behind us, and a fight ahead that not all of us may live through.*

Two well-hated bailiffs had been targeted, whose plundering and humiliation would please the flatlander peasants—bailiffs whose strongholds could be reached in something under a night's ride from forest, on trails and roads where their travel would raise no alarm. One was well west, a long ride through wild and forested hills. The reeve in that shire was why Three Forks had been fertile recruiting ground, a reeve who'd selected bailiffs as harsh and arrogant as himself. Macurdy had assigned Jeremid to lead that raid; as a third-year Hero, Jeremid was by far his most competent officer. The other bailiwick chosen was a lot nearer, but the ride through open lowlands was longer and seemed more dangerous. That was the one he was riding to now.

In his mind, Macurdy began to review again what he knew about the bailiff's stronghold. For whatever royal reason, bailiffs weren't allowed a stockade. What they generally had, or so he'd been assured, was a fence not much taller than he was—a miniature palisade of stout locust stakes set in the ground, with stout oak posts every six feet or so—presumably white oak so they wouldn't rot. The whole thing was tied together with a growth of thorny rose vines so no one could climb it. There'd be a padlocked wagon gate in front. He hadn't seen padlocks in this world, but he imagined them as large and heavy. Next to it would be an access gate just wide enough to lead a horse through, barred on the inside, and guarded. Inside were large fierce dogs. This bothered Macurdy more than guards, though his men didn't seem concerned.

For the life of him, he couldn't think of anything he hadn't considered, but he kept reviewing doggedly. The biggest unknown at the village, it seemed to him, was how many men the bailiff would have on hand. Bailiffs were allowed eight arms-men on their permanent payroll, but at tax time they hired as many as thirty toughs from other bailiwicks to help collect the taxes. Would they be hanging around guarding the loot? His people seemed semiconfident they wouldn't, but the possibility troubled Macurdy.

Still, it seemed to him likely he'd get the loot and out of the village without serious losses. Then, instead of backtracking, they'd turn east. There was supposed to be an east-west road just north of the village, that would get them to the North Fork Road before midmorning. By that time the reeve would have been no-tified, and have his company on its way from his castle on the river west of Gormin Town. They'd be twice his number, better trained, better armed, and on fresher horses. Of course, by the time they caught him, their horses wouldn't be so fresh, but his own men would have been in the saddle, or working or fighting, since dusk the evening before, and their horses wouldn't have much run left in them.

The North Fork Road roughly paralleled the North Fork of the Calder River, with its stringer of woods. About an hour be-fore you reached extensive forest, the East Fork flowed out of the hills to join the North. There, Wollerda was to be waiting with two hundred men, to jump the reeve's company from behind when it had passed. Then Macurdy's platoon was to turn and hit it from the front. Between his force and Wollerda's, they'd outnumber the reeve's more than two to one.

Macurdy couldn't afford much delay at the village. If the reeve caught them before they'd passed the junction with the East Fork, they were in serious trouble. They'd have to abandon the loot, try to reach the forest and scatter. His people said not to worry, it wouldn't happen that way, and he'd nodded as if he accepted their assurance, but…

And finally, how well would his men perform? Would they hold ranks? Fight well? Would *he* make good decisions?

On top of it all, his mouth hurt where new teeth were push-ing through. Now he knew why teething babies fussed. New teeth! Weird, at his age. Apparently it was a side effect of Varia's magic to keep him young.

* * *

Macurdy could hear the village dogs almost as soon as he saw the village, their distant barking less insistent than that of the farm dogs they'd passed. *Bark bark,* pause. *Bark bark bark,* longer pause. Like Morse code, he thought. Houses hunkered darkly in the moonlight, with here and there something taller—barns and stables he supposed. Somewhere in there was the bailiff's stronghold.

His lips stretched tight over his grin. He felt better now, as if the immediacy of action was clearing away his nervousness. Quickening his horse, he caught up with Tarlok. "Keep it to a walk," he said, loudly enough for the men to hear. "They won't react so quickly."

At four hundred yards the village dogs became aware of them, and the barking spread quickly, gaining energy. Another wagon road crossed the one they were on; they'd take it eastward when they left. Meanwhile their present road took them into and almost through the village before they came to the stronghold, its fence looking solid and formidable in the darkness. The barking from inside was deep and raging, a sort of staccato roar that made him twitch.

His men knew their assignments and needed no orders. One group turned off on the near side, another rode past and turned off at the farther corner, each group with a packhorse carrying a ladder for laying against the fence, a ladder broad and strong enough for three men to cross abreast. Macurdy and the rest stopped in front of the gate and waited. If there'd been an outside guard, he'd disappeared. Meanwhile what were the inside guards doing? Their dogs were just inside the gate, barking like something out of hell. The whole village had to be awake by now, he thought, and for the first time wondered what would happen if the villagers sided with the bailiff. Traditionally, flatlanders and hillsmen had been hostile to each other, feelings dating from ancient wrongs occasionally renewed. The bailiff, on the other hand, was a present and continuing evil. But...

Then someone inside whistled shrilly, a signal to those

outside, and the dogs raced away from the gates, still raging. There were shouts from several points, and very close by, a man screamed. The barking thinned as dogs were killed. The access gate opened, and one of Macurdy's men looked out.

Macurdy trotted in with another group, and stumbled over a body; a gate guard, he supposed. He wondered if his people had taken any prisoners, as he'd instructed, or if they'd simply killed everyone they didn't know. There seemed not to have been any serious resistance. His attention went first to the wagon gate—a double gate, its two halves meeting in the center. They were barred—that was no surprise—but they were also fastened inside by a heavy, padlocked chain through two large eyebolts. And they needed them open, to get the packhorses back out when they'd been loaded.

"Slide the bar out!" he shouted. "Use it as a battering ram!" One of his men tugged on Macurdy's arm. "Captain! They had a bunch of tax girls shut up in a shed. What do you want done with them?"

He followed the man. The girls, four of them, had been brought outside. Macurdy judged their ages as being from twelve to perhaps seventeen. Even by moonlight they looked terrified. Two, seemingly the younger, were crying, their voices keening. He spoke to the one he judged oldest: "Tell them no one's going to hurt them. Tell them I'm going to send you all home."

Someone else came to him, to announce the bailiff was dead. "And Captain, we found a little casket in the house, full of coins—silver and gold!"

"Good. Tie it shut and load it on a packhorse."

Someone came to tell him the battering ram wasn't doing the job. They'd also tried using the ironwood pry poles Macurdy had had them bring along, to pry the gates up off the hinge pins, but the pin ends had been hammered, and the hinges wouldn't come off. Macurdy raised his head. "Someone bring an ax to the gate!" he bellowed, "and a torch. Right away!", and jogged to where the men had laid down their ram.

A sizeable crowd was gathering outside. Tarlock was talking to them. *Damn!* Macurdy thought. *If we don't get this gate open right now, we're going to look like a bunch of clowns to these people.*

"Captain! There's a guy here's got something he says is important."

"Have him wait! Where the hell is that ax?" As he asked it, a man ran up with one and handed it to him. Macurdy stepped up to the wagon gate, eyed the U-shaped padlock bolt, wound up and hit it as hard as he could. The body of the lock fell to the ground. He grabbed the chain, hanging loose now, and pulled it out of the eyebolts, then four of his men shoved the gate open.

The person with the important information was a boy of about fifteen years. He'd seen someone come out of his father's horse shed, leading his father's best horse, a man wearing the helmet of a bailiff's armsman. He'd mounted and ridden quietly south, headed out of town.

The outside guard, Macurdy suspected, on his way to notify the reeve.

The next man who wanted to talk to him was the village spokesman, the man voted by the villagers to represent them with the bailiff. He was agonizing over the tax girls. When Macurdy said he was sending them home, the spokesman blinked with surprise, then shook his head. "The reeve has already been sent an inventory. He will come here and take them back; hunt them down if he must." The man looked worriedly into Macurdy's face. "It's best if you can take them to a safe place."

For just a moment the two men traded gazes. *Shit!* Macurdy thought, *things must be bad here, if he's putting his trust in us.* "All right," he said, "but two of them are children. Bring me a woman of the village, a strong one who can ride well, to look after them. And tell your people why we took them."

He turned away from the spokesman and went to check on the loading of the packhorses, to make sure they weren't overburdened. They'd have to keep up with the saddle mounts. But the spokesman, he became aware, was following him anxiously. "Excuse me, Captain," he said. "Did you know the reeve has stationed his company at a farm on the Great Road? They are more centrally located there, and also much nearer to us. If they arrive before you leave..."

"*Tarlok!*" Macurdy bellowed, and the man came running. Briefly they talked, and given this new information, Macurdy decided they had little or no chance of making it via the North Fork Road. They'd have to go back the way they'd come, and as quickly as they could. He sent one of his best riders, a youth who might have weighed 120 pounds, on the bailiff's best horse, to find Wollerda and let him know the trap was aborted.

Hurriedly they then finished loading the pack horses with two bags each of wheat. The tax girls and the woman who'd tend them were helped onto five of the bailiff's horses. Another townsman had told him there were tax cattle in a paddock just outside town, and Macurdy sent men to get them. The guards there had fled too, it turned out.

When they rode north out of the village, they had not only the pack string, but the tax girls, and three village youths who insisted they wanted to join the rebel band. And eight of the tax cattle. The rest had scattered, and there was no time to round them up.

* * *

When he rode away from town at the head of his column, Macurdy already could see faint dawnlight along the eastern horizon. Before long he could see a mile or more. No one seemed sleepy, and from time to time they trotted their horses. The sun rose, and began its daily trip. They passed farmers on the road or at chores, or in the fields—men and women who stared worriedly at them, and kept out of their way. Meadowlarks challenged each other in liquid notes, while marsh hawks soared over the hay fields, watching for rodents. Gradually the morning warmed, but remained less than hot; the humidity was low and the breeze pleasant. It would be easy, Macurdy told himself, to think the danger was over, if there'd been any in the first place. And maybe it was over, but that seemed unlikely.

After a bit, Blue Wing found him. "Macurdy! Macurdy!" he cawed, and Macurdy, pulling off the rutted, hoof-packed road, waited while the column passed. Waited for what he was sure was bad news. A rail fence bordered the road there, and with uplifted wings, the great raven braked to land on it. Carrying on a conversation in flight was difficult.

"You are not where you told me you'd be!" he said accusingly.

"I found out things I hadn't known. The North Fork Road's too dangerous. We'd have been caught."

"They're coming! Many more of them than you! And they're riding faster! You'd better hurry!"

"Thanks. We'll go as fast as we dare, but we don't dare wear the horses out." *And the pack string may start to gallop, and the cattle. That'll use them up fast.*

The cattle, Macurdy decided, were the most dispensable, but he'd keep them as long as he could. "How close have they gotten? Have they forded the creek with the brushy banks?"

Blue Wing looked at him exasperated. "Most of the creeks around here have brushy banks."

"The creek with brush that comes up to the road. The next to last creek we crossed between here and the village."

"I'll see." The bird flexed its legs, and launched itself with a whoosh, whoosh of powerful wing strokes. Then Macurdy urged his big gelding into a canter, to catch the head of the column again.

The great raven was back before many minutes, and Macurdy and Tarlok pulled off the road while the column passed. Their pursuers had crossed the creek, Blue Wing said, were well past it. Tarlok shook his head. "We won't reach the forest before they catch us. Not unless we leave the pack string behind, and the cattle. And if we do that, they'll say they beat us—that we quit. That we're scared of them. And the story will spread."

"Right." *And it'll kill the optimism people have been feeling. Especially these guys.* He turned to Blue Wing again. "There are two places ahead where we rode through woods last night, after we left the forest, but I couldn't see well enough to know what it's like there. Go take a look for me."

Again the great raven left, then returned. Blue Wing always described things differently than a human would, but it seemed to Macurdy there were opportunities in those woods.

He chose one squad and told them what he had in mind for them. The country here was higher, sloping generally southward, and where the woods farther south were mostly in scattered small blocks, here they were irregular, oriented on irregularities in the terrain. It was midmorning when Macurdy came to a broad shallow draw, with a creek running through it flanked by woods. By that time Blue Wing had swooped low a couple of times to urge speed; their pursuit was getting close. Looking back, Macurdy could see a dust cloud: the reeve's men. No doubt they were trotting their horses by intervals.

He and Tarlok kicked their own animals into a brief downhill canter, leading the column into the draw. When they were well into the trees, Macurdy and the squad he'd chosen drew up. Tarlok pulled off too, and called for the others to halt.

"Captain," he said quietly, "do you figure on staying here with them?"

"Yep."

"Best you leave me with them. Lose you, and the whole company will melt away like maple sugar in the rain. But lose me and folks will hardly notice."

"I'd notice."

Tarlok ignored the reply. "By now, everyone knows what you've done. You get yourself killed, and people from Gormin Town to Three Forks to the Saw Pit Valley will lose heart. While most of them never heard of me." Tarlok turned to the others and called out. "Men! Anyone here think the captain lacks guts?"

The chorus of nos was emphatic; there was even laughter, as if the thought was ridiculous. Tarlok nodded, satisfied. "Captain," he said, still loudly, "you don't need to stay here because it's more dangerous. What you need to do is ride on with the column, for the same damn reason."

The man sat easy in the saddle, eyeing his commander. Macurdy nodded, and without answering verbally, nudged his horse with his heels, passing the halted rebels to the head of the column. There he paused just long enough to call out, "All but Rensey's squad—move out!"

They rode. At the break of the draw, Macurdy paused. The

road had shrunk to little more than a broad, well-beaten trail, though there still were cart ruts. Looking back toward the head of the dust train, he could see the leaders of the pursuit column. After the last of his drovers had passed, urging the cattle with voices and staffs, he turned his back on Tarlok and the chosen squad. For the first time really aware of how these men looked at him.

It was a burden he hadn't recognized before. It seemed to him now he owed them at least as much as he owed Varia and himself.

* * *

When Blue Wing came back, Macurdy rested the column briefly while he took the bird's report. The reeve's company was on its way again, continuing the pursuit. Yes, some of the ambush squad had gotten out alive, riding upstream; four of them, he thought. (He could handle the smaller numbers well enough.) Some others had probably snuck away on foot. The reeve's company had lost more. Blue Wing concentrated, then guessed that "ten or more" horses or men had fallen.

More important than that, his pursuers had lost time. The picture Macurdy put together was that the initial flight of arrows had felled several. And instead of driving through, the soldiers had fallen back and discussed it; apparently they had little stomach for casualties. Finally they'd sent their own flights of arrows toward the ambush, but from long range, skewering dirt and trees. Meanwhile they'd sent out strong detachments to enter the woods above and below the ambush, and flank it.

Then the reeve's main force had charged again, and experienced no further archery until almost to the woods, when more men and horses went down at point-blank range. The rest rode into the woods and dismounted, presumably to kill or run off whoever had been shooting at them, instead of doing what they should: riding on through, continuing their pursuit. In fact, no one continued up the road until the flanking parties arrived.

It seemed to Macurdy whoever led them suffered from an acute case of stupidity, losing track of the objective.

Aloft again, Blue Wing spied their pursuers coming harder

than before, closing the gap. "All right," Macurdy said to him, "we'll hit them again at the next wooded draw. Go tell Wollerda what's happened. You'll probably get to him before the courier I sent on horseback."

According to Blue Wing's earlier report, the next woods was a broader band, also following a stream, and as Macurdy visualized it, not more than two or three miles ahead. Now, as he rode, he shouted his plan to his men, then let them pass and repeated himself to the packers and drovers.

All of them pushed their tired horses a little harder. This next stand, Macurdy told himself grimly, would be their last chance. If even a dozen soldiers kept going and caught up with the pack animals, the raid would turn into a fiasco that could wound the rebellion badly, perhaps fatally. Even reaching the forest didn't guarantee safety, if the reeve's commander was willing to follow. Then another thought came to him, easing his grimness. *They won't know there aren't some of us still with the pack train. If we down enough of them, they'll turn around and go back, especially if they lack the stomach for casualties.*

The second broad draw, when they came to it, was wooded clear across the bottom and on both slopes. He trotted his horse down into it, then sent the packers, drovers, and noncombatants on up the road. The rest of his men he scattered along the road by threes behind cover, their horses tethered farther back in the woods. He was depending on their pursuers being little smarter than before. Though they should have learned one lesson—to drive on through, or try to.

When he reached the far slope, he had only six men left to post, and it occurred to him he should have saved more for the upslope, when the soldiers' horses would have slowed. And the last six included the three lowlander youths. Unordered, they'd stayed instead of continuing with the train. He wondered if they had any skill with their bows. He'd heard flatlanders were forbidden to have weapons, which meant they'd had little practice. But at point-blank range...He placed them behind a locust thicket where the road started uphill out of the draw, then led his last three rebels upslope to the north edge of the woods, where he positioned them and himself out of sight, ready in the saddle, spears locked beneath their arms.

Now we wait, he thought, and promptly began to worry. He'd told his men to shoot horses instead of riders; particularly on the run, horses would be a lot easier to hit, and the soldiers probably wore mail byrnies. And if a horse went down in the thundering column, its rider was likely to be disabled anyway. But how many of his rebels would do it? These hillsmen valued horses, treating them well for the most part. And how well could they shoot, through gaps in the trees and undergrowth at galloping horses? Of course, the horses might not be galloping. He'd assumed the enemy commander would speed his column up through the woods, like running the gantlet, and by starting the gallop downhill on the far side, it wouldn't be so taxing. By the time they approached him, of course, they'd have slowed. It would kill horses already tired, to gallop uphill.

Minutes passed, then he heard the rumble of hooves. Coming down the far side of the draw at a gallop, he supposed. There was no shouting from either soldiers or rebels. In his mind he pictured falling horses, other horses falling over them, while others veered past.

Still the sound approached. He edged out far enough to peer down the edge of the road, and saw the foremost horsemen starting uphill, now at a slow trot. "Not yet," he cautioned. "Not yet...Not yet...*NOW!*"

The four of them spurred out onto the road and charged downhill. The soldiers' spears were in their saddle boots, out of action, for this was something they hadn't imagined. The foremost tried to swing aside, but there was no room for maneuver, no shoulder to the road; just packed dirt, then trees. And others were pressing from behind; they piled up instantly.

The shock of his spear striking a soldier nearly unseated Macurdy, and as his own horse braked staggering, he swung out of the saddle. He and his three rebels drew their heavy sabers, and hacking and hewing, attacked those horses and riders trying to get past the pileup. Then the soldiers began to dismount, sabers in hand, and he found himself bellowing *"Break off! Break off!*"

Then tried to break off himself, but a thick-waisted arms-man pressed him, red-faced with rage, and he had to kill the man to disengage. It took several long seconds. Then he ran. After a minute, realizing he wasn't pursued, he slowed to a rapid stumbling walk, panting from exertion and excitement, to continue upstream among the trees. Wondering whether or not the reeve's soldiers had caught the packstring and cattle.

* * *

One of his rebels came along on horseback and pulled Macurdy up behind him. After a bit they rode out of the woods, and stopping, dismounted to let the horse rest awhile and graze. Then they continued on foot, leading the animal. More mounted men joined them, jubilant over the fight, and Macurdy allowed himself to feel a little optimistic.

Two hours later they were in unbroken forest; by evening they'd reached camp. The packstring was already there, and the cattle and tax girls. Everyone cheered Macurdy, acting as if he was some kind of genius. Melody kissed him soundly, while rebels grinned.

And Blue Wing was there, with news. He'd reached Wollerda before the mounted courier, and Wollerda, instead of going home, had led his company westward across the North Fork Road, pushing their horses in a forced march on country lanes, still determined to engage the reeve's company. Blue Wing had served as scout.

After Macurdy's second ambush, the soldiers had turned back. They traveled slowly, partly because of their wounded, and partly because some were riding two on a horse. Wollerda jumped them at a draw south of the first ambush site. Numerous soldiers were killed there, and most who fled were caught. Prisoners were disarmed, and their horses and boots taken. They trudged south barefoot, carrying the news.

It took two more days for all of Macurdy's survivors to straggle in, some of them wounded. All but eleven of the original fifty-two made it, and Tarlok was unscratched. The flatland teenagers weren't among them.

Meanwhile a messenger arrived from Jeremid. He hadn't been pursued, and was on his way with grain, twenty-three head of cattle, and several flatlander volunteers. He expected to bring more recruits from Three Forks. The only fighting had been brief, at the bailiff's stronghold; none of Jeremid's men had been killed, and only three wounded.

Macurdy sent a detail south with pack horses to strip the dead armsmen of byrnies and weapons.

Rebel morale was out the roof. Even their worrywart commander was feeling pretty good.

Chapter 27: Of Truth and Lies

One of the nicest things Macurdy returned to was Melody. She didn't try to take him to bed, just ate breakfast and supper with him, teasing him hardly at all. She seemed reconciled to his marriage vow, though why she remained interested, he didn't understand. Meanwhile she had a women's tent set up to accommodate the tax girls and their guardian, as well as herself and Loro, the excaptive from the Orthal days.

Three days after Jeremid returned, Macurdy sent him with a full company to hit the reeve's stronghold. The guesstimate was fewer than twenty of the reeve's company would have returned from their pursuit of Macurdy and his raiders. His fort would be thinly defended, unless he'd been reinforced. Not the usual stockade, its walls were stone, twenty feet high.

Jeremid had known what to use for opening the gate; he just hadn't expected to find one so handy. Scarcely two hundred yards from the fort was an inn, its taproom catering to armsmen. A new stable was being built for it, and there, waiting to be raised, was the forty-foot roof beam. Now he wouldn't have to tear down someone's roof to get his battering ram.

It took him less than half an hour to have an A-frame made from other timber at the site, meanwhile sending a platoon around behind the fort with bows and scaling ladders. These then threatened an attack on the rear, holding defenders there, while construction laborers and stable horses, protected by byrnie-clad Kullvordi shieldmen, dragged first the A-frame, then the ram to the fortress gate.

It took a bit to set things up, and despite the shieldmen there were casualties, but within half an hour the gate had given way. The fort's defenders—fifteen escapees from Wollerda's massacre, plus a dozen household guards—surrendered promptly.

Jeremid didn't send all his men inside. Four galloped off toward Gormin Town, two miles east, to the tent camp outside its partially burned palisade wall. Less than an hour later, a mob was forming outside the fort, shouting they wanted the reeve turned over to them.

Meanwhile Jeremid's men had commandeered the thirty horses in the reeve's stable, and across their backs put rope slings. Then they loaded most of them with tax grain brought in from the bailiwicks—two heavy sacks of wheat, and two of the much lighter oats per horse. A few, instead of being loaded with grain, would carry all the weapons his men could find.

At that they could load only a relatively small portion of the grain stored there. Then a long line of grinning townsmen was let inside, and the rest of the grain began disappearing out the gates on their shoulders.

The reeve and his chief deputy were turned over to a local "committee of justice." The A-frame was already being converted to a gallows, and briefly the committee discussed whether to "merely" hang them there, or to flog them and then hang them. Meanwhile Jeremid had a newly named "rebel X" slashed in the forehead of each captured soldier, with the warning that any of them recaptured in Gurtho's service would definitely be executed. His advice was to leave the country till the rebellion was over, to avoid being forced back into service.

Jeremid had arrived none too soon, a captive told them. A count's platoon was expected the next day, with a wagon train to haul the tax grain to Teklapori.

* * *

After the raid on the bailiffs' strongholds, Kithro had begun operating a ration supply system for the rebel force, assessing the hillsmen a lighter equivalent of the royal tax, which he pointed out was no longer being collected, a tax which would be used to secure and support their own freedom.

Meanwhile, problems of logistics and space had worsened.

The camp was well-located for security, but with the growth of Macurdy's Company, it had too little pasture for its horses and cattle. And with more and more recruits, supplying them over rough trails by packhorse was becoming impossible. So they moved to a much more accessible area, taking over public pasture accessible by wagons from the North Fork Road.

There crews were detailed daily to build longhouses: cutting, dragging, and fitting logs, splitting out roof planks and shakes, and building mud and stick fireplaces. The hillsmen were handy and cheerful at almost every sort of work, and morale remained strong. Partly because they were busy, partly because they could see so much progress, and partly because they had no doubt that with Macurdy's leadership, this rebellion was going to succeed.

Gurtho, and not "the flatlanders," had become the focus. Macurdy continually made a point of their common cause, Gurtho being hated by both. As for what they might do when Gurtho had been thrown down, time would tell.

* * *

Meanwhile, Gurtho had embarked on a campaign to gain the affection of the Teklan commons, throwing a large and costly party in every town and major village to celebrate the eleventh anniversary of his coronation. It might have worked to a degree, if people hadn't had to sit through a speech, ill written and mostly ill read, on the virtues of King Gurtho and the dangers of the Kullvordi. If the virtues of Gurtho had been left out, it might have worked to a degree. As it was, both peasants and townsfolk failed to cheer it. What they cheered were the whole roast oxen, the bushels of roasted early corn, and the barrels of beer. Local musicians were paid to play, and people danced till they dropped from beer or exhaustion, or found a partner to have sex with in the shadows.

And of course, none of the counts, reeves, or bailiffs told Gurtho the speech had failed, for Gurtho himself had written it, and he was highly sensitive to criticism. He'd had Idri read it in advance, for her opinion, and had she been honest with him, it might have been repaired. But she'd praised it. For Sarkia's ambassadrix sent two couriers a week to the Cloister, and received two. And the Dynast had quietly changed her position regarding the existing king of Tekalos.

* * *

Eight-Month was well underway, and the rebel ranks grew daily. One day after lunch, Macurdy, Kithro, Melody and Jesker began to go over the table of organization together. Wollerda had a raid in mind, a lot bigger than anything they'd done before, that required cooperation from Macurdy's Force. As yet, though, Macurdy had no units larger than companies—108 officers and men each, following the Ozian system. All in all he had 736 officers and men, as of the day before, but in his opinion, fewer than half had had enough training to be sent into battle, with many of those being only marginally ready.

So they sat sweating in Eight-Month's humidity and heat, cooking up a short cohort that could be brought to full strength later.

They were hardly well started when a courier galloped up. "Major!" he called as his feet hit the ground. (Macurdy had promoted himself with the growth of his command.) "There's two women want to see you! Out by the main road! They're Sisterhood. Got three guards with them, Sisterhood guards I think; their uniforms aren't Teklan."

"Did they name themselves?"

"No sir."

Macurdy's lips thinned. Not Idri, he guessed; not Gurtho's queen. She'd know better. One of her people then. "Tell them I'll meet one of them beneath the oak on the road in. Just one of them. The rest wait where they are."

"Yessir. Oh, and the boss of them—so pretty I couldn't believe it—she's got a tomttu riding up behind her with his arms around her waist. What I wouldn't do to be in his place!"

Flustered by Macurdy's hard stare, the man remounted and rode away. It took the conference about ten minutes more to agree on principles and begin assembling, on paper, a cohort of four companies: three of spearmen and one of bowmen (though all would carry bows and quivers); bowmen required less training. Then Macurdy, leaving the others to finish the job, started for the paddock. Aware Melody was following, he stopped and turned. He could see the concern on her face and in her aura.

"Do you think one of them is your wife?" she asked.

He shook his head. "She'd have identified herself."

"Is there—any danger one of them will spell you?"

"They can't. If they try, they're dead meat. Varia told me once spells aren't worth much against other magicians. Between her work with me, and Arbel's, there's no danger of it."

Melody's expression didn't change. "I'll come with you. With a squad."

His grim face softened, smiled. Reaching, he touched her face. "I'll go alone," he said, then continued to the paddock to catch and saddle his horse.

As he left, her hand went to the cheek he'd touched. But he hadn't changed her will. She commandeered a squad of men and followed him. Not disobeying his order, she told herself. They'd follow only to the far edge of the woods and watch from there, ready to leave when he turned back. But if there was trouble…

* * *

Alone except for the tomttu, whom she'd moved around in front of her saddle, Liiset watched Macurdy ride toward her. She hadn't seen him since he was a gangling fourteen-year-old. Even at two hundred feet she could see the change in him, not only in his hard bulk—that was the least of it—but in the way he sat, the way he held his head. And as he neared, his steady gaze and the strength of his aura.

I wonder if Varia ever even imagined him like this, she thought. She could see why men gathered to him and followed his orders. Briefly she wondered if he'd think she was Varia.

He answered that when he halted his horse, fifteen feet from her. "Who are you?" he said. "What do you want here?"

She answered in English. "I'm an envoy from the Dynast, come to speak with you. You're looking well, Curtis."

He said nothing to that, nor did he look surprised. He simply sat waiting.

"Varia would be proud of you if she knew. A year and a half ago you were a farmer on Farside, knowing nothing about Yuulith. Not our language, our ways, our weapons—not even our existence. Now you lead an army here."

He answered in Yuultal. "Why did you come to me?"

"To offer you vengeance."

"Vengeance? I could make a good start on that right now," he said, and half drew his sword.

"Vengeance on the wrong target gives no lasting satisfaction. And if I let you, would you cut me down? I'm not only Varia's clone sister, I'm her favorite, her best friend."

He reseated his sword. "You're Liiset then."

She nodded. "I'm Liiset."

"So who am I supposed to take my vengeance on?"

"The ylver. Those guilty of the rape at Ferny Cove; she told you about that. And most particularly on an ylf named Cyncaidh."

"On the ylver? Idri's the one who stole Varia from me. If she was here, I'd show you vengeance."

Liiset had no doubt he meant it. *Sweet innocent Curtis has changed,* she told herself. *Idri's impulsiveness at work. Well, no doubt it's for the best. Sarkia seems pleased, and she doesn't make many mistakes. Though if she could see him now…* "I appreciate your feelings," Liiset said, "but you'd have a hard time killing her if she were here. She has considerable powers."

"Bullshit. If she was here, she'd be fly bait. I guarantee it." He paused. "What's this Kincaid to me?"

"There is much you don't know yet. Much you couldn't know." She put her hand on the tomttu's shoulder. "Curtis," she said, "this is Elsir. Elsir, tell Commander Macurdy what you know of my sister."

The tomttu didn't read auras; he simply saw them and got an overall impression, discerning little of their detail. This man it seemed to him, was dangerous. "My lord, she knocked at my door in the forest, limpin', and with a pack on her back. It was the start of dusk, and I'd just built a fire in my fireplace. I'd have asked her in, but she'd have had to squeeze through the door on hands and knees, and couldn't have been comfortable inside anyway.

"So I asked what I could do for her, and she told me she'd run away from her Sisters, hopin' to reach a gate and go back to her Curtis. To you. She asked if I knew of any dangers ahead, and if I could spare her somethin' to eat.

"I told her I knew of no dangers that she didn't; there always bein' dangers in the wilderness. And that I'd be glad to spare her a loaf, and a small mess of greens. Not enough for a tallfolk, but all I had."

He shrugged his small shoulders. "She lay down to rest on the grass then, and I'd just come back out with the loaf—when there they were, a dozen ylvin devils trottin' up the path! Soldiers on a spyin' mission, I have no doubt. Had they been ordinary humans, they'd never have seen my hut, nor your Varia lyin' by it, for I'd protected it with a spell. She'd fallen asleep, and when I opened my mouth, their leader broke my spell with a wave of his hand, the same leavin' me paralyzed and without speech. It wasn't till one of them raised her by the hair that she wakened."

He feigned a shudder. "They questioned her, strikin' her repeatedly, and—did other things to her. And when they were done, all of them, they tied her weepin' and bleedin' across one of their horses, and rode away laughin'. But before they left, I heard the others call their leader Cyncaidh."

Macurdy's tight lips writhed, and Elsir thought his small heart would stop. "Myself they left where I lay," he went on, "and I don't mind tellin' you I was frightened half to death. Any fox that came along, let alone wolf or catamount, could have had me for supper! But about midnight the paralysis wore off, and I managed to crawl inside and bolt my door.

"The next day, another Sister came along, on horseback with a guardsman, and I told them what I'd seen."

Liiset spoke then. "That was Berit, another of our clone. She'd been tracking Varia, and turned back at once. Then Sarkia sent a master of concealment and tracking to follow the ylver's trail, north to the Big River and beyond. He followed them through the Marches and into the empire itself. And far to the north, to Cyncaidh's palace by the Northern Sea.

"He took his life in his hands then, and allowed himself to be seen. After weaving a spell to resemble an ylf, a spell adequate to fool the common ylver. If one of the more powerful had seen him though…

"He'd ask one of them an innocent question or two, then ask someone else a question based on what he'd learned from the first. Repeating this a few times, he learned how she'd fared: Cyncaidh had made Varia his slave and concubine, holding her up to public mockery."

Macurdy's aura had thickened and darkened with anger. And there was more which Liiset couldn't read. "They're evil, Curtis," she finished. "And that's where your vengeance belongs: on the ylver and Cyncaidh."

His voice was husky when he answered. "And why not on your Sisterhood as well? It was you who stole her. Took her away by force, otherwise none of this would have happened. I've talked with an Ozman who said her hands were chained when she arrived. And Idri's man tried to rape her."

Liiset took his hard stare easily, though clearly he knew more than Sarkia or any of them had realized. "That's true," she said. "And Idri herself killed him for it. But Idri acted on her own in stealing Varia. And Sarkia punished her for it, saying Varia owed us nothing, that if anything, we owed her. But Curtis, the ylver killed so many of the children and babies, at Ferny Cove…We needed her. That's the truth Idri acted on."

Macurdy had studied Liiset while she spoke, seeing more than she thought, and his intensity had eased. "If this Kincaid lives by the Northern Sea, what is this vengeance you offer?"

"We talked King Gurtho into offering peace and autonomy to the Kullvordi, if they'll join his army. He's concerned about you, afraid you might defeat him."

"What's that got to do with vengeance on the ylver? By spring, Gurtho will be finished anyway."

"It's not just your vengeance we're interested in. The vengeance *we* want is for Ferny Cove, and that requires a large and powerful army. The crudest tribal chief would not have committed on us the brutalities they did, not on such a scale, and they savaged the Kormehri almost as terribly, earning fear and disgust through all the Rude Lands.

"We've put embassies now in every kingdom but Kormehr, from the Eastern Mountains to the Great Muddy, and from here to the Big River. As Gurtho's general, you and Sarkia can put together a powerful army between now and next spring. With you as general, for somehow you've become a skilled and inspiring commander."

Macurdy looked thoughtful instead of angry. "And how far do you expect me to lead it? Not to the Northern Sea."

"It will be enough if you take it through the Marches and into the empire. The Marches are ready to kick free their ylvin shackles. At best they'll join with us. At the very worst they'll take no part on either side.

"Simply to march into the empire itself will redeem our honor and be vengeance enough. Into the empire far enough our allies can loot ylvin manors and take their wealth home with them. And by then the ylver's slaves may rise up. If they do, who knows how far we may go. If not—" Liiset shrugged. "The emperor will be glad to negotiate, and we'll demand Varia back. He'll give her to us, too. Then she'll be free to go back with you to Farside, or you can live here together, with far more wealth and power than you could ever have there."

His gaze penetrated, then switched unexpectedly to the tomttu. "Elsir, where was she captured?"

"Why—near the head of Tuliptree Creek, on the Laurel Notch Trail. But that's far off east of here, in the Dales at the east end of the Granite Range."

Macurdy held the tomttu's eyes a moment longer, then returned his gaze to Liiset. "I'll think about it for a week or so," he said. "Send one of your guards as a courier then."

Without another word he turned his back on her, nudging his horse into an easy trot. Liiset and Elsir watched him ride away, and from his perch in front of her, the tomttu spoke quietly. "Ah, lady, it's an evil thing we've done, lyin' to him like that."

"It's not lying, Elsir, if it helps someone grasp a larger truth."

The small face turned to hers. "A lie's a lie, whatever the intention." He turned again and watched Macurdy disappear into the forest. "And he knows I lied."

"No, he was suspicious to begin with, but by the time I was done, he was convinced in spite of himself. And if it's any consolation, consider that we gave you no choice."

"There's always a choice, lady. Even if the choice is death."

"That was no choice for you, Elsir. Macurdy is no friend of yours. You never saw him before."

"And may I never see him again, for I have greatly wronged him." He looked up at Liiset again. "I believe my people know more about the ylver than yours do. There are good and bad among them, but they've been much less evil to my people than humans have. Cyncaidh would not have made me do what your Dynast has."

Liiset was touched by the tomttu's courage in speaking as he had, and laid a light hand on his shoulder. "Believe me," she said quietly, "the Dynast's spy did follow her, all the way north. And her captor's name is Cyncaidh. It was necessary that you lie a little." *While I told only the truth, the truth according to Sarkia, who lies when it suits her.*

She helped Elsir move behind her, his long fingers clutching. When he was settled, she turned her horse and started back toward the North Fork Road. Macurdy had left with some intention in his mind, something that presumably would take a week, and she wondered what it was.

Chapter 28: Truth

Macurdy unsaddled his mount at the paddock, and told the herd boss he wanted five strong horses readied for himself and one other by mid afternoon, two with pack saddles; and oats for twelve days. He glanced upward in irritation as he spoke, for rain clouds were moving in. Then he strode to his headquarters tent, where one of his runners, a fourteen-year-old, jumped to his feet.

"Find Captain Tarlok. Tell him I need to see him right away."

"Yessir!" the boy said, and took off at a trot. Macurdy fiddled briefly with supply records, occupying himself until Tarlok appeared. "Is there anyone in camp who knows the trails to the Granite Range, and the Dales?" Macurdy asked. "I need a guide, on a mission only I can do. For information."

Tarlok frowned. "How long will you be gone?"

"Until I've learned what I need to know; it could be a dozen days or more. I'm leaving Jeremid in charge."

Tarlok nodded. "Blue Wing could probably guide you."

"He's needed here to scout or courier for Jeremid."

"Well then, there's a lad named Fengal in my company, as good in the woods as any you'll find. He's only eighteen, but grew up wild. His mother is Indrossan, from someplace called Hemlock Cove. She died two years ago, and his dad came back to North Fork, bringing the lad with him."

"Good. Have him sent here, with his horse, bedroll, and saddlebags."

Tarlok nodded and got to his feet.

"Another thing," Macurdy said, and told him to expect a

courier from the Sisters. He was to lodge and treat the man as a semi-prisoner, treat him well but not allow him to talk with people. "I'm accepting him as a courier, not a spy," Macurdy finished.

Tarlok acknowledged and left. Then Macurdy sent another runner to find Captain Melody and send her to his tent. His third runner he gave instructions that Fengal, when he got there, was to wait.

He was packing his saddlebags and bedroll when Melody arrived, her tunic rain-spotted. "What is it?" she asked.

"I'm going on a trip, with just a guide, and someone needs to know what I'm doing and why." He paused. "The Sister I talked to told me where Varia is. Supposedly. Where she is and how she is."

Melody nodded soberly.

"But I'm not sure how much of it I believe. She had a tomttu with her, to tell me part of the story, and both of them were lying part of the time."

"Lying? How do you know?"

"When Arbel worked with me, I learned to see what he calls auras, like a cloud of colored light around a person. I can see yours right now. And with practice, if you see them clearly and you're paying attention, you can tell when someone's lying."

Melody stared at him. "She told me Varia was captured by an ylf named Kincaid, and taken north into the empire—way north, to the Northern Sea. That part she believes, but the rest she's not sure of. The tomttu said he saw her capture, and they both know that's a lie, but at least he saw her."

He paused. "First I'm going to where the tomttu said it happened. Maybe I can learn something. Then—I'll do whatever comes next."

"What about us? Your army?"

"I'm leaving Jeremid in charge. He's as good as I am." He chuckled then, getting up. "In some ways, anyhow."

She didn't smile. "When are you going?"

"As soon as I've talked to Jeremid. Half an hour."

She stepped forward, hugged him hard and kissed his

mouth, then stood back and looked at him. "Come back to us, Macurdy," she said. "Come back to me, anyway."

He didn't chuckle now. "I will," he said. "I promise." And wondered again why she felt the way she did.

* * *

When Macurdy got back to his headquarters tent, Fengal was waiting. He was a lean youth of middle height, with a look of wiry strength; overall he made a good impression. Macurdy told him what he needed him for, while a courier went to get Jeremid, who arrived inside of five minutes. Macurdy told him he was leaving, going on a mission only he could carry out, that would probably influence what they did next. And that the Sisterhood wanted an alliance—that a courier would arrive from them in a week or so. Tarlok would take care of the man.

Then he and Fengal went to the cook tent for cooking gear and rations, and rode out of camp in another sprinkle of rain.

* * *

For five long days they rode eastward, ignoring stealth, Macurdy picking up bits of woodscraft from Fengal. The days and nights were showery, with occasional brief hard rains, yet they made only a minimal camp at night, sleeping where dusk found them, spreading their oiled tarp over a quick frame of saplings. They left their cooking gear unused, their only fire at day's end, to dry or semi-dry their clothes, though they did bake potatoes in the embers. They were up at dawn with the thrushes and wrens, and ate in the saddle: jerky and hard bread, their jaw muscles aching from it, and cold baked potatoes. And occasional wild apples, worm-tunneled but edible, for on the old burns where they stopped to graze their horses, there sometimes were apple trees. Macurdy wondered how they'd come there.

Finally they came to what Fengal said was the Laurel Notch Trail, used much by wildlife and seldom by man or horse. They turned off on it, northward now instead of east. Beside it, in a small wet meadow, they found horse bones gnawed and scattered; by a troll, Fengal said. Macurdy wondered what had become of the rider. As they continued north, he felt a growing tension, an excitement. He felt more alert, it seemed to him, than he'd ever been before.

Now he watched for a tomttu hut; any spell of invisibility or protection should have dissipated, but if it not, Macurdy had no doubt he'd see through it. They crossed through Laurel Notch, and some time later passed a spring, the headwaters of the Tuliptree. Still no hut. He wasn't surprised. According to Maikel, tomttu didn't settle in the wilderness. They only traveled, or at most sojourned in it.

What he did find were human bones, the thigh bones long. A tall man then. They weren't splintered and sucked dry by a troll, nor scored by the teeth of wolf or bear or some large cat. Its bones had been cleaned by smaller teeth, weaker jaws, beaks and worms and bacteria.

Its chest had been cleaved by something long and sharp, possibly a sword.

He hadn't found it by the path. He'd felt an impulse to leave the trail, to snoop behind a laurel thicket not far away. Whoever had killed this man had dragged him there out of sight.

"Not all that old," Fengal said, his voice subdued. "Old bones weather gray. These are still pretty white."

Macurdy knelt, picked the skull up, looked into the empty eye sockets—and began to tingle. Abruptly disorientation struck him, then momentary confusion followed by an instant of blankness. Yet he didn't lose consciousness, just his sense of identity and time, looking through eyes not his own, as if he were someone else. It seemed he was striding uphill, breathing deeply, less alert than usual. Sensing nothing peculiar, nothing dangerous. Then a bowstring twanged, and there was a sudden, shocking impact, a horrible penetration that drove the strength from him, and he fell to his knees, staring down at a feathered shaft protruding from below his breastbone. Ambush! He was aware of men in buckskins, with swords, and strove to rise again. Felt a smashing blow cleave his rib cage, then looked down at his body from a viewpoint perhaps ten feet above it.

But only for a moment. For instead of being absorbed with the reality of his death, his attention went to the action around him. Besides the cluster of men, there was his captive—filthy and with her hair stubble-short—staring at his broken body, her mouth round with shock. One of the ambushers held her from behind, gripping her shoulders, keeping her from falling.

Until the sword struck, there'd been sound—hoarse breathing, feet on earth, the bustle of movement. Then it nearly stopped, silent as stone, the action below him in ultra-slow motion, speeding gradually, until there was sound again, slow and hollow. "You're all right, you're safe now," one of them said to the woman. The man who held her upright. "We know who he was, and who you are. A tomttu told us. He was anxious for you. Your tracker had been only hours behind."

During that short speech, the speed normalized and the sound became natural, as if his mind had adjusted to a new input channel. Now, while still experiencing the murdered man's perceptions, he was aware of his own identity as Macurdy, heard and watched the sequence that followed, heard the tall ylf tell of Ferny Cove, saw the woman set on horseback. Saw them ride away, out of sight. There'd been no questioning, no blows, no rape, no harshness.

Became aware of someone shaking his shoulder, and for a moment saw nothing, then awoke to present time, lying on soggy forest mould among the bones. It was Fengal who knelt beside him. "Major! Major! Are you all right?"

Macurdy groaned, pushed himself to hands and knees and got up, his speech slurred. "Yeah, I'm all right. I—saw the whole thing: what happened here, what the dead man saw. It's what I came for. Now I know what I need to know."

The youth stared at him in awe, not doubting. He knew his commander was a magician, had seen him light fires. They went to the sound of water over stones, dug dry punk from inside a hollow tree, built a fire, and for the first time used their griddle, making corn cakes.

* * *

Macurdy remained preoccupied, as if still assimilating what he'd learned. When they'd eaten, instead of starting back to Laurel Notch, they lay down to nap. His last conscious thought was to wonder where Varia was, and what she was doing.

Chapter 29: Sea Gate

Cyncaidh and Varia had stayed up late the night before, bundled warmly on a balcony, holding hands while she watched her first aurora, a marvelous play of lights shimmering and pulsing not just in the north but over the entire bowl of sky. Then they'd slept late by their standards, and busied themselves for a time while the sun climbed the sky, he entering various records into a ledger, while she read more imperial history.

By late morning the temperature was perhaps 75 degrees Farenheit, almost hot for late summer on the Northern Sea, and they'd left the manor on foot, hiking a graveled path that led through half a mile of forest to the shore. Cyncaidh wore moccasin-like step-ins, soft, bleached-linen trousers, a low-crowned, untrimmed hat of straw, and a jacket-like shirt with sleeves only to the elbows. Varia wore a short kilt over knit tights, and a knit top with long sleeves. Held by the beauty of the morning, neither of them said much as they walked.

A gap opened in the forest, widening as they approached the beach, broadening the view ahead. The sky held not a cloud, and the air only a light breeze. The dry haze of autumn was three or four weeks in the future, and the air was crystalline, showing the icy water sapphire-blue to the horizon. Well offshore, a string of rocky islets angled northeastward across the view, providing perspective and composition.

They had no escort. Cyncaidh himself carried the basket that, besides a picnic, held jackets in case the wind picked up. A servant had preceded them by half an hour, with blankets, oars and sail. He'd installed the sail, seated the spar, then left by another path, to avoid imposing on their privacy.

The small cove was sheltered on the northwest by a low spine of basalt, the ghost of some ancient volcanic dike, ground down, rounded and smoothed by glacial ice. By contrast with its near blackness, the dry beach sand was surprisingly white, and audible as they crossed it to the small dock where a fourteen-foot skiff was tied. There was a minute of verbal exchange, cheerful and mostly purposeful. Then Varia crouched in the bow with a short boat hook, while Cyncaidh pushed off from the dock and manned the oars, leaning into them and pulling out into the smooth-surfaced cove.

She put down the hook and watched him row, noting the sinews in his long forearms, his lean athletic lines. It was a body that little by little, these weeks, she'd learned to appreciate and love. It differed from Curtis's, as their personalities differed. Both men were muscular, though their lines and proportions were not at all alike. Both were strong-willed, too, but not bull-headed—considerate, able to give way—and both were sweet and loving. But Raien was—not wiser but more intellectual, and in bed a smoother, more skilled lover. Curtis relied more on his reactions. Of course he was nearly thirty years younger, but the difference was more basic than that.

Her life, she told herself, had been rich after all, in gifts as well as trials.

It occurred to her she'd been comparing the two men, the loves of her life, something that would still have been impossible, unthinkable, just four weeks earlier. The changes in her viewpoint and emotions still sometimes surprised her. They'd been sneaking up on her over the gentling, strengthening weeks of intermittent sessions with Mariil, sessions that healed both mind and spirit. And she'd discovered she could think of both men without guilt or any other discomfort. Or compulsive assignment of precedence. Each loved her, and she loved both of them.

But Curtis was in another world. He'd hardly fit in this one.

Not that healing was complete, it might never be, but it seemed to her it had gone far enough she could face whatever she needed to face, without being overwhelmed or experiencing great grief. And Mariil had seemed to thrive on helping, as if she too was getting a new lease on life. The techniques she used, certain others also knew, A'duaill for one, and increasingly herself, with Mariil her teacher. But Mariil, Varia recognized, had the greater healing talent. It was a healing not imposed like surgery, but internal, replete with tears and laughter, the realizations and decisions her own, though guided and facilitated by Mariil's insights, skilled questions and instructions.

Commonly the effects weren't noticed until, the next day or week, Varia realized certain responses had changed, that this and that reaction and attitude were different than they had been. And in the process of opening and cleaning out old mental lesions, more than the effects of abuse were dealt with: old learning and conditioning were also exposed. Some of which she cancelled or modified, and some she reaffirmed within her newly evolving world view.

Under the gentle pressure of sun and sea breeze, her eyes had closed. Now she became aware that the skiff's movement had smoothed, and she opened them again. Cyncaidh had stowed the oars and raised the sail, and lost in her thoughts, she hadn't noticed. He sat grinning in the stern with the tiller under his arm, while the breeze bellied the linen. The cove was behind them; his eyes were on her. She smiled back at him. He could be boyish too, a boyishness different than Curtis's.

* * *

Cyncaidh watched her eyes close again. Lovely, lovely eyes, he told himself, in a lovely face relaxed and lightly tanned. Looking at her, he felt strong, strong and able. And lucky.

He loved her tan. It was a rare ylf that tanned. Among them, protection from sunburn was a subtler function of ylvin physiology. Which could be overloaded, thus the ylvin fondness for hats and body covering against prolonged exposure. He loved her legs, too, admired them, preferred them bare; their clean lines and smooth muscularity excited him sexually. And he loved her slender waist; her back, well-muscled instead of bony; her easy flexibility. The strength that still surprised him when her passion released it, and the dance exercises Sisters were taught, to maintain their endurance and beauty. She did them daily now, elaborating on them, she told him; said she intended to make an art form of them.

Dancing she excited him, and relaxed she soothed him. As now. He wondered what she was thinking behind her closed lids, and hoped it was of him.

* * *

Varia opened her eyes from time to time, to see Raien in the stern, and the shore falling farther behind. With a following breeze and little draft, they moved briskly.

This was the third time he had taken her boating. The first two trips had been overnighters, exploring the coast first westward, then eastward. Bypassing fishing hamlets, they'd skirted wild beaches, snooped cliffs, and explored the lower reaches of streams, Raien unstepping the spar and using the oars when necessary. She'd loved the places he'd shown her; some looked as if no one had been there before. They'd poled up one rocky gorge which in spring, he said, was a raven rookery, loud with the croaking of the large black birds, hundreds of them, their nest trees clinging to rocky walls, where fledglings gripped the branches determined never to let go despite the noisy urgings of their elders.

Sometimes she'd rowed. At first her request had surprised him, but he'd overridden his cultural conditioning and let her take the oars. More than once, she'd told him, she'd rowed Will's rented boat on the Mustoka River, while Will worked the water with his casting rod, for bass. Raien had frowned, and she'd asked him why. He'd been trying to visualize it, he'd said. Trying to visualize Will, and Varia's marriage to him. He had less difficulty, he told her, visualizing her life with Curtis, though he wasn't at all sure his images were realistic.

It seemed to her she handled the complications of her past more easily than Raien did.

* * *

With the following breeze, sailing was simple, and Cyncaidh's attention remained largely on Varia. Her lovely eyes opened only for seconds at a time. Her aura, he noted, was almost as calm as if she slept; whatever she was thinking was pleasant but unexciting. Shortly they drew even with the nearer islets, and he angled toward the one they'd picnic on. Most were mere skerries, bare black rocks overswept by waves in the heavier storms. Three, however, had developed shallow soils and a bit of vegetation, while the largest had not only scrubby aspens and birches, but a small stand of black spruce, complete with nesting birds that fed on bearberry and bilberry, and the seeds of other dwarf shrubs that grew there.

"Here comes our picnic ground," he said, and opening her eyes, Varia turned to see. He lowered his sail and manned the oars as they coasted in, letting the tiller trail, pulling up beside a natural dock he knew, a finger of dark basalt. The bow slid gently onto shiny black shingle rock, and Varia, stepping onto the natural dock beside her, pulled the bow farther up, grounding it securely. Someone in the past had driven a steel picket into a crack, and Raien tied up to it, then took the picnic basket ashore, putting it down higher on the narrow beach, where he spread their blankets on the sand.

"It's a little early for lunch, don't you think?" Varia asked.

He grinned down at her from his six-feet-four. "I thought we might do other things. Here where we have both privacy and sunshine."

She grinned back, put her arms around him and raised her face. "What did you have in mind, your lordship?"

He began to show her, his hands in the back of her tights while they kissed. After a minute they lowered to their knees, then lay down, dallying and petting, and before long made slow love in the sunshine. Afterward they had their lunch: coarse bread, apple butter, cheese, and a flask of beer cooled in the shallows. When they'd eaten, he led her into the shade of the spruce grove, and spread the blankets on feather moss. There they made love again, then dressed and napped, and afterward sat in the beached skiff to finish the contents of the basket.

He pointed northeast, out at the farther islets. "You can see the farthest two from here," he said.

The non sequitur remark sharpened her awareness. His aura reflected watchfulness, a certain tension; he had something to tell her, and wasn't sure how she'd take it. Puzzled, she looked where he pointed.

"Out there is the Sea Gate."

"Sea Gate?"

"There's a gate there, presumably to Farside. I thought you should know."

Frowning, she stared at him, not yet angry.

"It's called the Sea Gate because it opens over the water between the last two skerries. And it's different in other respects. The other gates I've heard of open when the moon is full, at midnight or high noon. This one opens irregularly during periods of northern lights, and apparently stays open for hours at a time. Perhaps days sometimes.

"Long ago, one of my great-great-uncles went through in a boat to see what was on the other side. He planned to see, then return at once, and several boats waited for him. Only his boat came back, overturned but intact. Twice since then volunteers have gone through, and not even their boats were seen again."

He paused, looking at her. Her expression had turned thoughtful. "I thought we might go out there," he said. "After last night it may be stirring. We can feel it if it is. Would you like to?"

She answered only after a long moment's lag. "Has anything ever come through from the other side? Besides your great uncle's boat?"

"Not that we know of. Nothing seen floating, no bodies or anything unusual washed up on the beach."

She couldn't correlate the geography of the two worlds well, but it seemed to her that Lake Superior might be on the other side, and told him so. He nodded thoughtfully. "If it is, it's probably cold, like the sea here. And if the arrival there is rough, rough enough to overturn you…"

"I've gone through both ways," she said. "Coming through to this side is the most violent, but going through the other way, you never know what position you'll arrive in. Hardly ever on your feet."

"I've read the same sort of thing. Do you want to sail out there? Close enough to feel if anything is happening?"

Again she frowned thoughtfully. "I suppose we should. I don't know what we'll accomplish—nothing, probably—but..."

He nodded, and after they'd stowed their things in the skiff, she got into the stern. He untied the painter, lifted the bow free of the shingle rock and pushed off, Varia holding the tiller. Then he raised the sail and sat down by her in the stern. Approaching the gate site, they felt nothing unusual, and after circling it, turned to tack their way shoreward, slowly, for the skiff had little draft, and only skeg and rudder to bite the water.

* * *

On their way back to the cove, a slender ship passed them, a Sea Swallow, swift and graceful, its mast unseated, driven by long oars. The colors of an imperial courier fluttered at the stern. When the couple reached the manor, the courier met them, giving Cyncaidh a sealed envelope, while a troubled Ahain hovered unnoticed in the background. Slitting the envelope, Cyncaidh read the message, then turned to Varia. "Lochran has died. The Chief Counselor. Unexpectedly. The Emperor wants me to come at once, with the courier."

Ahain interrupted. "Your lordship!"

Cyncaidh turned, noticing him now. "Yes?"

"Lady Cyncaidh lost consciousness this morning after you left. Lord A'duaill says it's a stroke. He doesn't think she'll live out the day."

Cyncaidh's jaw clenched, and he turned to the courier. "I'll stay till my wife can either travel or has died. Meanwhile I'll have preparations begun."

"As you say, Lord Cyncaidh."

"Meanwhile I'll look in on her, and discuss her condition with Lord A'duaill, my wizard and healer. You and I can talk further after supper." He turned to Varia, who stood white-faced, her knuckles between her teeth, not at the unexpected move but at the report of Mariil's stroke. "Lady Varia, perhaps you'd care to come with me."

She nodded. "Of course, your lordship."

They went together to the second floor, to the east wing, and went in. Mariil was still unconscious. They'd been there only minutes when her spirit aura flickered out. She was dead.

Chapter 30: Confrontation

The ride back from Laurel Notch had been like a vacation. It had even been sunny, with only two showers, hard but not prolonged. Macurdy talked more with Fengal as they rode, and learned more from him. It seemed to him the youth had been born a woodsman, that at eighteen he knew and understood more about the forest than many who'd spent a lifetime in it. So they'd been gone a full eleven days when they arrived back.

Liiset's courier had arrived, but Macurdy made no immediate use of him because the joint operation with Wollerda's force was almost ready. Jeremid briefed him on it, and two days later they rode out at the head of four companies of eager hillsmen.

Macurdy wondered at their easy willingness to face an armed enemy. Some had seen friends die on the tax raid; a few had been wounded themselves. Jeremid commanded; he was more familiar with the situation and plan. Macurdy went along because he felt he should, and to inspire the men, who seemed to think he was invincible.

The town they rode toward was the seat of the county which included the western hills, and for that reason, the count who ruled it had been reinforced with a company from four other counties. Jeremid had learned this from spies. And the castle had been warned of the rebel approach; Jeremid and Wollerda had seen to that. Now if the count would cooperate…

He did, sending out all but his fortress company to meet and destroy Macurdy's rebels.

Meeting this much larger force, Jeremid ordered a retreat, which then seemed to lose order and turn into a rout. The count's force pursued them, until the soldiers, more or less strung out, cantered past a river forest. There Wollerda's 1st Cohort had concealed itself the night before, and charging out, confused and disorganized the soldiers. At the same time, Macurdy's rebels turned on their pursuers.

The soldiers fought without enthusiasm and at a severe tactical disadvantage. Rather sooner than the rebel commanders had expected, royalist trumpeters signaled surrender. The rebels disarmed the soldiers then (they'd drilled even that), taking byrnies and shields, swords and spears, bows and quivers. And hundreds of horses, on some of which they loaded the loot.

In Kellum, the county seat, well-led teams looted the homes of officials, taking coins, silver, jewelry, scented wax candles and other valuable goods easy to convert to cash to help pay the costs of the growing rebel army. Beyond that, looting was forbidden, a forbiddance assisted by limited opportunity. This caused grumbling, but nothing serious, for Macurdy, Wollerda, and their officers lived among their men and pretty much as their men, commonly eating with them, the same food in the same portions.

The count refused to surrender his castle, and Wollerda and Macurdy left it unassaulted. It was much more formidable than the reeve's had been. Wollerda's and Macurdy's strategy, at this stage of the rebellion, was to demonstrate without question their military effectiveness, enhance their supply situation, and bleed and demoralize the royal army. In all of which they'd succeeded.

What they hadn't done yet was force the king to commit his personal cohort. They weren't ready for that—not outside the hills—and they knew it. It was why they hadn't challenged the count who ruled the eastern hills: He was much nearer Teklapori.

Meanwhile they held the initiative, and their morale was stronger than ever, despite casualties. Their training had been much briefer, and most rebels lacked byrnies, yet in open combat they'd beaten the count's soldiers, who supposedly were superior to those the reeves could field. The advantage had been rebel spirit and vigor, and better leadership.

* * *

It was after his return to camp Macurdy sent Liiset's courier with a written message to her, expecting a quick response. The first half dozen days of waiting were no problem; after all, he'd made her wait. Meanwhile no further offensive actions were planned. Morale no longer needed them, and it was time to prepare for what seemed a certain royal response, either diplomatic through the Sisterhood, or military—a concerted offensive to destroy the more accessible Kullvordi villages and crush the spirit of rebellion. Macurdy and Wollerda had a strategy to meet that too, one that called for preparations, as many as they had time for. Time negotiations could help provide.

Jeremid had already designed a shield that was neither Ozian nor Teklan, and could be made rapidly. Rebel losses would have been substantially less if they'd had them before and been trained to use them. Macurdy and Kithro had developed a system for their manufacture. Kithro contracted with a range of providers: woodsmen who felled large shagbark hickories and cut them into roughly three-foot-long sections. Carpenters who split planks from them, and trimmed and planed them to the proper dimensions and weight; tanners who produced leather from bull hides, cutting it to size and shape; and smiths who made iron bands to strengthen them, and iron bosses and hooks to make them dangerous.

Among the hillsmen, tanners were the glue makers, too. They'd made the glue to glue pieces of hickory together, because suitable single-piece shields were tricky to make, and gluing would often be necessary. Bull hides would then be stretched over them, shrunken into place and hardened. Finally iron cross bands would be riveted on, and bosses and hooks added. And when squads got their shields, they'd begin a simple shield-training regimen borrowed from the militia at Wolf Springs.

Payment for shields, as for much else, would be in captured silver, army horses, and if need be, chits.

* * *

After the sixth day, though, the continued lack of response from Liiset began to gnaw on Macurdy's mind. What was the holdup? He'd gotten the impression they were eager. Did they plan a surprise? Treachery? Something to give them leverage?

* * *

Meanwhile, on Macurdy's fourth day back from the Dales, Kithro had come to his tent, where he sat talking with Melody and Jeremid after supper. "Fengal's been telling an interesting story," Kithro said.

"Oh? What's that?"

"The story of what you found over below Laurel Notch: a set of human bones. He said you dropped to your knees, looked into the eyes of the skull, yelped a cry, and fell on your face in some kind of trance."

"I can't vouch for the yelp, but the rest sounds about right."

"He says you lay there for quite a while, babbling like someone in their sleep. Talking in other people's voices about ylver and Ferny Cove and other things that meant nothing to him. And woke up mumbling about having seen everything that happened there."

"Huh! I never thought he'd talk about it. I'm disappointed in him."

Kithro shook his head. "A boy like that, seeing and hearing what he did, couldn't be expected to keep his mouth shut. And he's done you a favor—done us all a favor—because the story's spread all through camp."

Kithro paused. "My people used to have shamans. Till Gurtho's great-grandfather executed most of them; them and their progenies. Claimed they'd been a source of agitation. After the slaughter, the people lost faith in shamanism and the favor of God. There's a few villages still have someone who calls himself a shaman, but their magic doesn't amount to much. For healing, we depend mostly on old women with a few simple spells and knowledge of herbs.

"Then you came around and made fire with a wave of the hand, and grew new teeth. Now there's this story of Fengal's. The men have gotten excited about it. They consider you a shaman warrior for sure, now. A shaman of power."

He looked meaningfully at Macurdy. "I thought you ought to know," he said, then left, the others watching him go.

"Hmh!" Melody looked accusingly at Macurdy. "You didn't tell me any of that." She turned to Jeremid. "Did he tell you?"

"Nope." He raised an eyebrow at Macurdy. "How about it?"

Macurdy grunted. "I guess I should," he said, and began.

* * *

On the eleventh day, he had an answer that explained the delay: Sarkia had come to Tekalos, was at the palace with a company of guardsmen and one of Tigers. She wanted to meet with him outside Gormin Town, at the junction of the North Fork Road and the Valley Highway, in four days.

The message arrived in midafternoon. Haltingly he read it to himself, and again after supper to Melody sitting across from him, and Jeremid at his elbow.

"Sarkia," Melody said when he'd finished. Her face was very serious. "She's supposed to be the greatest sorcerer in the world. Don't go, Macurdy."

"Do you think she'll put a spell on me? Catch my soul in a bottle? Scramble my brain?"

She peered at him unhappily. His expression was calm, matter of fact. "She'll try something," she answered.

He remembered how easily Varia had influenced him, that night in Indiana. But it hadn't been sorcery that got him in bed with her, though it *had* gotten him to her house. And he'd been an innocent then, ignorant, a psychic virgin. Yet even so, in the morning he'd had second thoughts about marriage, objections she'd had to answer.

"I've got the talent," he said, "and I've had some training. She can't make me do what I don't want to." *And there's a lot at stake here for me. There's no other way I can hope to get Varia back. None at all.*

"These Tigers," Jeremid said. "Are they as good as I've heard, do you suppose?"

Macurdy shrugged. "I guess that depends on how good you've heard. Varia mentioned them once; she thought they were the best. Savage, highly skilled, and stronger than other men. And they won't be tentative like the people we've been fighting."

Jeremid gestured at the paper lying on the table. "Why do you suppose Sarkia mentioned them in her message?"

"I can only guess. Maybe she wants to scare me. Added to Gurtho's cohort, just a company of Tigers could make a big difference. Even without Gurtho's cohort, a company of guards and one of Tigers makes it too dangerous to take a cohort south to capture her. Not that I would."

"They could be to keep us from rescuing you, if she takes you prisoner," Melody said.

"True. But it doesn't feel like anything to worry about."

"You're going to go regardless of what we think," Melody said. "Are you going to take a bodyguard? Besides the escort who'll ride down there with you? Someone who'll be beside you during the meeting?"

Macurdy grinned at her. "Who have you got in mind?"

She grinned back ruefully. "Me."

"If I was going to take someone, it would be you." *And let them think maybe I have a new love. Let them feel they have to offer more. But if something does go wrong...*

"But you're not taking anyone."

"Right."

"What about Wollerda?" Jeremid asked.

"That's the next big question." Macurdy plucked a sheet of paper from a small stack, then reached for his inkwell. "I want you to write a message to him, for me to sign."

* * *

Blue Wing carried the message and brought back Wollerda's answer: Macurdy could meet with Sarkia but make no final commitment. If he failed to return, Wollerda would accept Jeremid as Macurdy's successor. If Macurdy's Force elected someone other than Jeremid as their new commander, Wollerda was not committed to work with him, although he'd consider it.

Usually Macurdy slept well, and the night before leaving was no exception. The officer of the guard wakened him at the first light of dawn, and he got up feeling exhilarated. He and his escort of ten men were in the saddle and on their way before sunup. Despite the unknowns, Macurdy's sense of strength and confidence grew as he rode. He wasn't euphoric or ecstatic, just alert and confident, sure of himself. This would work out.

The state persisted through the morning.

Near midday, in the distance, he could see the inn at the crossroads. He'd assumed Sarkia intended to sit down with him there, but almost as soon as he made out the inn, he saw what looked to be a tent, a large pavilion erected on the other side of the North Fork Road. Shortly a dozen men were riding northward toward him at a brisk trot, and after closing the distance somewhat, he halted his escort to wait. The reception party stopped a hundred feet away, sitting its horses in precise ranks. Two of its members rode the rest of the way at a sedate walk. Macurdy had no doubt they were Sarkia's rather than Gurtho's. Mounted on beautifully matched black horses, they wore black uniforms with polished cuirasses and helmets that, from where he sat, looked to be silver. The two who came to meet him wore clusters of long scarlet ribbons from their helmet peaks.

"You are Commander Macurdy?" one of them asked. He showed no hauteur, despite the rebels' rough clothes and casual ranks, nor did his aura show anything like scorn.

"That's right."

"If you are prepared to meet now with the Dynast, I am instructed to conduct you to her. A meal is being prepared for her and yourself. Your men will eat with us if you wish, or they can eat apart."

"Where do I meet her? In the tent?"

"In the pavilion. Correct."

"My men will eat at the inn. I'm ready to meet the Dynast, the sooner the better."

The guard officer nodded. "Follow me, please." Macurdy turned, called an order, and his men fell in behind the guardsmen while their commander rode beside his guide.

The pavilion, as he neared it, impressed him. Its vivid red, white, and gold roof and wall panels were brighter than he'd have thought possible. (He'd heard that among other things, the Sisterhood made expensive dyes.) Segments of the walls had been rolled up for ventilation. As he drew even with the inn,

Macurdy gave another order and his men turned off, riding to the stable beside it. His air of confidence was so strong, so clean, that none of them faltered in leaving their shaman/commander unguarded. He turned the other way and followed his guide to the pavilion, where he dismounted, handing over his horse to a guardsman-orderly.

At the entrance, the leader of his escort reported to a Sister that this was Commander Macurdy. The woman disappeared inside, and two minutes later another came to meet him. For just a moment he thought she was Idri, whom he'd seen but once. But neither aura nor eyes fitted what he knew of her. An Idri look-alike, he realized, as Liiset looked like Varia.

"Commander Macurdy," she said, "the Dynast will see you now."

"Will she? I'm here at her invitation, and I've had a long ride. I need something to drink first, and take a crap."

The woman's aura hardly reacted to his deliberate crudity. "Drink and lunch are both served in the Dynast's room," she answered. "Oran will show you to the guards' latrine."

Macurdy didn't really need to go. He'd been establishing his independence. Following Oran into the latrine, he released the little water he'd accumulated. There were washbasins on a trestle table, bars of white soap, and pitchers of water. On a fresh bar, the name "IVORY" was stamped. From Farside then, probably brought from Ferny Cove.

When Oran returned him to the entrance, the woman still waited. "I don't know your name," he said.

"I am Lariin," she answered.

"Lariin. Right. I'm ready."

He went inside with her, feeling primed but at ease, and found himself in a corridor walled with golden yellow cloth. Its ceiling was much lower than the roof, to help keep the pavilion from overheating in the sun, he supposed. At the corridor's end he found the Dynast in what he decided was a reception room, rather than her living quarters. Its furnishings seemed too fine for even such a tent as this: a handsome table, waxed and burnished, with inlaid squares of some pale wood, paler than white oak, alternating with what he recognized as black walnut: a mosaic of old ivory and rich dark brown. There were matched, upholstered chairs as well, and a small buffet. The room was open to the west, the direction of the breeze.

Three women got to their feet as he entered. Liiset. And Idri; that was a surprise. And what could only be the Dynast herself, looking physically no older than the others, though there could be no doubt she was. And somehow it seemed to him he had little to fear from her.

Her gaze was inscrutable, her aura calm. "So you are Curtis Macurdy," she said.

"I am. And you're Sarkia. And that ugly bitch on your right is Idri." He turned his eyes to Varia's kidnapper. "If I'd known back in Evansville what kind of vicious sow you are, I'd have wrung your humping neck and stuffed you down a privy."

His gaze shifted to Sarkia. "Just so we understand each other."

Idri flushed, her aura flaring dark with anger. Sarkia was coolly amused. "It seems I needn't worry you won't speak your mind; Varia did an outstanding job of selecting her second husband. Had I been consulted, I'd have left her on Farside, with the understanding she provide us with litters by you. There'd have been no difficulty in leaving one of each to gladden your personal lives there.

"But I can hardly condemn Idri, for if she hadn't stolen Varia from you, I'd never have had this opportunity. You are even more—far more attractive to me as a leader and general than as the sire of children. Although my Sisters would be more than happy to provide you with company, if you'd like. I'm sure you'd find any of them quite accomplished in bed. And Liiset is much like Varia; she could warm your nights nicely until you get your wife back." The Dynast eyed him appraisingly. "No? Perhaps Idri then. You could consider it revenge of a sort, and she's notoriously good in bed."

Sarkia's face and voice were pleasant and matter-of-fact. Even her aura showed no particular emotion. But beneath it all she was cold. *She could pet a kitten,* he told himself, *then throw it in with the hounds to see if they'd kill it.*

"That's not the kind of vengeance I had in mind," he answered, then turned the conversation to business. "Liiset told me you want an alliance. Between you and Gurtho and the rebels, with me as your general. The fact I'm here now tells you I'm interested. But I owe my rebels more than just fighting. What they want is their independence, and I won't accept less for them."

"What would your Kullvordi think of playing a special role in the kingdom of Tekalos, with you as its king? And Varia your queen. I have no doubt you can produce worthy heirs, and your hillsmen could provide your royal guard; indeed the core of your army."

Macurdy's eyes were steady. He didn't trust the Dynast yet, even on a provisional level. "You sketch a nice picture," he said. "Where would the Sisterhood fit in it?"

"We want the opportunity to produce and nurture a new race, free of the empire's threat. For that, we need all the realms from the Green River Valley to the Big River united in an alliance. And for any such alliance to persist and be truly strong, the kings must be strong and able, ruling without constant serious injustices, and the rebellions, and wars between kingdoms, that grow out of those injustices."

"And Gurtho?"

"Gurtho has helped bring us you. It seems that was his function. His talents are few and his weaknesses a liability. Once we have an alliance, we will dispose of him."

Macurdy nodded. *She's cold as ice,* he thought. What he said next took them both by surprise. "You mentioned vengeance and Idri. Have her killed now, in front of me, and we'll talk alliance."

Sarkia's face froze, shocked ugly. "I will not!" she hissed. "There are limits!"

Ah! Even to your self-control. "Limits? Good! That's what I needed to know. All right, let's look at the military and political possibilities. If the prospects seem reasonable, we can discuss how to go about things."

* * *

They met for three days. Idri was always present, her hatred

of Macurdy suppressed and controlled but always there, showing in her aura. Perhaps, he thought, Sarkia didn't trust her to be
with Gurtho in her present frame of mind.

Each evening Macurdy returned to the inn and his escort,
and dictated a summary message for Wollerda. One of his guards
wrote it; Macurdy could read Yuultal, laboriously, but its spell-
ings were phonetically somewhat obsolete, and his own quite
nonstandard.

In the morning, Blue Wing carried it to Wollerda. And each
evening, Blue Wing brought Wollerda's answer. Wollerda was
leery of the Sisterhood, but as long as the discussions were exploratory and no commitments were made...What he'd like was
an agreement that removed Gurtho without more killing, or a
minimum of it, but invading the empire he considered out of the
question. It was altogether too strong for that.

On the other hand, Wollerda considered a defensive alliance among the kingdoms very desirable. And while negotiations were in progress, the rebel armies were growing, arming,
and training.

Chapter 31: Dialog

There was a quicker route between the two rebel bases than the long rugged way through forested hills. And with their improved military position, and the abeyance of hostilities, the commanders now took that route from opposite ends, to meet at a tiny, out-of-the-way flatlander village. At what passed for an inn, but was more of a local tap house with a single room for occasional travelers. Macurdy hired it, and he and Wollerda sat across a table from each other, Wollerda's aide at one end taking notes, and a pitcher of sassafras tea at the other. Two companies of fighting men lounged outside, and guards were stationed at the door.

"Invade the empire!?" Wollerda asked. "She's crazy. It's larger than all the southern kingdoms combined, has a lot more people, and it's far better organized. Each of its dukedoms— there's probably fifteen or twenty—has an army maybe as large as Gurtho's; better trained anyway. Then the emperor has the Throne Army, probably five times as large, and there are garrisons in the Marches."

He peered intently at Macurdy. "And you said?"

"I agreed to talk to you about it. What I want to do now is look at all the factors. What about the Marches? The empire conquered them and holds them down, and I suppose it taxes them. What if they revolt when we march in?"

"Unlikely."

"Why unlikely?"

"I suppose Sarkia thinks they will."

Macurdy nodded.

"Sarkia believes what she wants to. I've only been in two of the March kingdoms, but that's two more than she has, I have no doubt. And they were conquered, true enough, but oppressed? Under imperial hegemony, they've grown richer, their conditions of life are improved, they rule themselves better, and they no longer fight each other. There are probably resentments, maybe some with good cause, but the people I did business with—merchants and prosperous farmers—like things the way they are. I expect the rest don't feel too differently.

Macurdy pursed his lips. "What armies do they have?"

"The March kingdoms? Militias. Of volunteers. My impression is, they don't take it seriously. They know, even if Sarkia doesn't, the empire will protect them. So they don't consider themselves threatened."

"What about the ylvin garrisons?"

"What I've read is, one fort in each March kingdom, with a cavalry cohort stationed there."

"And how ready do you suppose the empire is for war?"

"Hmm. Probably not very. But it could get ready fast enough, if it felt threatened."

Wollerda peered intently at Macurdy. "You've said this is desirable because it would unite the southern lands. And it is desirable, even if it's temporary, because once it's been done, it'll be easier to do again. So I'm in favor of union in the form of alliance, if the terms are right. It can discourage the empire from another attack, perhaps more ambitious than the last one. But to actually invade it?" He shook his head.

Macurdy sipped tea. "Suppose we didn't reach the empire itself." Taking a thick rectangle of folded linen from his tunic, he spread it on the table between them, a map of the empire and the Marches, that Kithro had gotten him. "Suppose we only got to here," he said pointing.

Wollerda examined it critically. There were two tiers of kingdoms in the Marches. The southernmost were the so-called Outer Marches, its kingdoms bordering the Big River. North of them were the Inner Marches, bordering on the empire. Macurdy rested a large fingertip on the northern tier. "If we only got that far before our momentum was blunted, it would still cause a hell of an uproar."

Wollerda looked at him thoughtfully. Macurdy went on. "If, with Sarkia's help, we brought in all the kingdoms along the Green River between the Eastern Mountains and the Muddy, and all those between the Big River and the Middle Mountains…"

Wollerda shook his head. "Not enough. The emperor could bring a bigger army against us. Bigger and better."

"How quickly? Would the Throne Army be bigger than ours? Or would he have to wait until the ducal armies arrived? And how long would that take?"

Wollerda shook his head disapprovingly. Macurdy continued. "They'll hear about us getting ready, but how seriously will they take us? According to Sarkia, the kingdoms south of the Big River have never united to do anything."

His gaze was intent now. "Imagine the dukes meeting with the emperor in Duinarog." He pointed at the ylvin capital, on the river between the Middle and Imperial Seas. "Might it run about like this? 'Mister Emperor, the Marches have their militias. Let them fight the southerners; it's their land and their responsibility. And if they can't manage, you've got enough soldiers yourself; that's what we pay taxes for. Besides, those Rude Landers will never get across the Big River. They'll be fighting each other before that.' " Macurdy looked quizzically at Wollerda. "Like you said, it's a big empire, and most of those dukes would have a long way to march, or ride. Hauling weeks of supplies with them, supplies they probably don't keep on hand in the first place. Supplies it would take awhile to round up. And think of the expense!

"When—if—we actually cross the river, then they might start taking us seriously. But meanwhile we ought to go through those militias like corn through a goose." *Or will we? Suppose they turn out to be like the Ozian militias!* "The imperial garrisons might give us a bad time, but they're isolated cohorts, one here and one there. The emperor would probably get the Throne Army moving pretty quickly, but even they'd have a long way to come, unless he'd already moved them south."

His finger moved across the Inner Marches. "We ought to get this far, anyway," he added, pointing to a town labelled Ternass, on the main route between the Big River and Duinarog. North of Ternass was a zone well marked with symbols for marshes or swamps. A major road was shown crossing it, but God knew what it was like. "Far enough to shake things up in the empire, not to mention the Marches. Far enough they might negotiate in good faith to get rid of us, but not far enough to get caught with those swamps at our back."

Wollerda sat with his chin in one hand, lips pursed. "Possibly. Or the dukes might be right. It's hard to imagine getting allied forces to operate as an army."

"In that case," Macurdy answered, "we wouldn't invade." He changed tack then. "How solid is the empire? Sarkia says the dukes fight each other sometimes."

"They have in the past. But I don't think there's been any fighting between dukes during the fifteen years of Paedhrig's rule. Or before it for quite a while."

"But some pretty serious political fighting?"

"I don't really know. Historically there've been rivalries, bickering, political factions, and grudges between dukedoms. And the factions have internal squabbles. But I have no doubt at all they'd unite solidly against invasion.

"Furthermore, it could result in a counter-invasion that could ruin us here: the Quaie Incursion five-fold. It might even result in conquest, with the Marches expanded south to the Middle Mountains."

Macurdy frowned thoughtfully. "Suppose we say our strike northward is a punishment for—what did you call it?—the Quaie Incursion. Especially for Ferny Cove. That seems to be something the ylver have strong disagreements about. It got Quaie fired from the army and kicked off the Imperial Council."

Wollerda stared. "How do you know? Is that something Sarkia told you?"

Macurdy shook his head. "I made a trip, awhile back. To the headwaters of the Tuliptree River, to check out a story the Dynast's ambassadrix told me, and another one told me by a tomttu she had with her. I couldn't be sure what was lies and what was truth, so I went to look. That's where I found out about Quaie, whom I'd never heard of before. And what happened to him for what he did."

Wollerda's frown was back. "How could you learn things like that on the headwaters of the Tuliptree?"

Again Macurdy sat briefly silent. "I guess I'd better start from the beginning," he said, then told Wollerda what the tom-ttu had said about Varia's capture, and what Liiset claimed had happened afterward. And about his trip to the Tuliptree and what had happened there, to him and to the tracker who'd been bringing Varia back to the Sisterhood. And finally what he'd heard the ylvin commander, Kincaid, say.

"And there's no way I could have imagined it. I didn't know enough."

Wollerda wasn't just frowning now. He frowned thoughtfully. "Cyncaidh. There is a Cyncaidh, an important noble. That's all I know about him. But it's hard to imagine an ylvin aristocrat in buckskins, scouting through the Granite Range."

He paused. "And you want this invasion just to get your wife back, right? Have you thought of the blood it'll cost?"

Macurdy nodded soberly. "But if there weren't any Varia, and never had been—if I'd been born in these hills and was in this rebellion for only the reasons you are—it would still look like something to think about seriously. Knowing what I know now. It's all of a piece with an alliance that could make the southern lands stronger. And richer.

"Look at it like this. If you were king of Tekalos…"

"It's you the Sisterhood wants as king," Wollerda countered.

"I'd rather you have the job than me, and I don't think it makes any real difference to Sarkia. It was just part of her pitch to win me over. She doesn't read me—understand me—as well as she thinks; probably there are things she refuses to look at, possibilities she can't admit to herself. And if you were king of Tekalos, the country would be a whole lot better off, because you're a lot smarter than Gurtho, and you're not greedy, and you look at people a lot differently than he does.

"Whatever may be wrong with Sarkia, she wants the southern lands strong and prosperous, so she can have peace to breed up the Sisterhood the way she wants. Which might not be all that bad. She's marrying the kings to Sisters, to strengthen the alliance and ensure the royal successions."

Wollerda studied Macurdy. *He's more than a fighting man and magician,* he told himself, *and more than shrewd. He's deeper than I imagined. And a child of fate, by the look of it. And the Dynast just might have some good intentions after all.*

"But the only way to form an alliance," Macurdy was saying, "is to give it a reason that seems real and strong—compelling—to a bunch of kings and chiefs that don't usually look much beyond their own borders and the next tax collection. An invasion across the Big River might be what it takes. An invasion to teach the empire never to attack southward again. And I suppose we'll have to allow looting. That might even get the tribes to join us. If we could get Oz to send a cohort or two...

"We could set it up so assigned companies do the looting. One or two trains of plunder wagons from each kingdom and tribe under a central command, so they don't get into butchering, raping, and burning. We need to avoid the kind of hatreds Quaie cooked up.

"And because we'll make a big point, with our own people and those north of the river, that this is all to punish the ylver for the Quaie Incursion and the Rape at Ferny Cove. Put the blame on Quaie. Then if someone in the empire beats the drum for invading south again, those against it can point to the grief the Quaie Incursion brought them."

Wollerda shook his head, not in refusal but in the first stage of capitulation. "You've got it all figured out, haven't you?"

Macurdy shook his head. "I didn't 'figure it out,' exactly. That's just how it seems to me."

"You'll need to get every kingdom and tribe included in the alliance," Wollerda said. "Especially those between the Middle Mountains and the Big River, and they tend to be friendly to the March kingdoms. Enough to trade with them."

Macurdy nodded. "Getting their support will be the Dynast's

job. She has embassies in every royal court except in Kormehr. And even if she can't talk enough of them into an invasion, she can probably tie them into a defense alliance."

"A defense alliance won't get your wife back."

"True. But it'll be worthwhile for the kingdoms and tribes. And maybe—maybe I could be the ambassador from the Alliance to the emperor, and get her back that way. Maybe the emperor would make Kincaid let her go."

Wollerda stared. "Macurdy, you're..." He groped. "You're a man of faith. All right. I'll go along with further negotiations and see what you come up with. It scares me—makes my hair stand up—but it's a powerful opportunity, and we didn't get this far by being timid.

"Besides, remarkable things happen around you. You even grew new teeth! The Great God himself seems to be with you."

* * *

They sent a man down for ale, the first Macurdy had ever had, just a swallow, making a face at the taste. Wollerda agreed to an alliance, Macurdy negotiating for both of them. But Wollerda would need to approve. Macurdy would sign as military co-commander, while Wollerda would sign as co-commander and chief of the Kullvordi.

They shook hands on it, then Wollerda stepped back with a grin, his first of the day. "And now, Macurdy, I've got a gift for you."

Macurdy frowned. "I hadn't realized. I didn't bring one for you."

Wollerda laughed. "I knew you'd say that; you don't know everything about us yet. We have a custom that one doesn't reciprocate a gift; it's an insult to the giver. If you want to give something in return, it'll need to be after a decent interval. A few months, at least." He beckoned. "Come with me." Together they left the inn and walked to the paddock, where Wollerda climbed over the fence and started toward a tall powerful gelding with almost a stallion's neck. It watched him approach without trying to avoid him, though it tossed its head as if to run, or maybe turn and kick. Wollerda spoke as he approached it, took the halter with a hand and led the animal to the fence, where Macurdy watched.

"What do you think of him?"

Macurdy was ill at ease, suspecting but not entirely sure. "A fine horse. Spirited. Big and strong, good hocks to hold up in the hills—and looks like he could run. And big-barreled; lots of endurance."

"He's a stag, actually," Wollerda said. "I didn't cut him till he was two and a half. I was going to ride him as a stallion, to raise my standing with my neighbors, but he was too unruly."

Looking at Macurdy, the animal jerked its head, but Wollerda held him in, speaking soothingly. "He's fine now, broken with an easy hand by a Kormehri magician. From near Ferny Cove, actually, before bad things happened there. Anyway he's yours. If you're ever chased, he won't collapse under you." Wollerda chuckled. "Actually he's more a gift to the horse you've been riding; the poor beast's getting swaybacked carrying you."

Macurdy climbed easily over the paddock fence, and stood for a moment feeling mentally for the horse's mind. *Okay, old timer,* he thought to it, *you and I are partners from now on.* He reached out, took the halter with his right hand and stroked the long silky nose with his left. The animal's eyes neither rolled nor threatened.

"Does he have a name?"

"Whatever you want to call him. I call him Champion."

"I had an uncle on Farside two stones heavier than I am, and he had a saddle horse that carried him with no trouble at all. Not as nice an animal as this, but big and powerful. Had a strain of Belgian in him—back home that's the heaviest draft breed—but a gait smooth as silk. And a really good disposition; my brother and I used to lead him to the fence and climb onto him from it, and he never minded a bit. Carried us wherever we wanted, together or separately. Uncle Will named him Hog. In our language, of course. Said he was strong as one." Macurdy cocked an eyebrow. "I told Frank that when I grew up, I'd have a horse like Hog, but until now I never did. You wouldn't feel insulted if I named him that, would you?"

Wollerda laughed again. "I won't. I don't know about him."

Macurdy looked the horse in the eye. "How about it? All right if I call you Hog?"

The animal snorted.

"He's telling you it's the kind of name a flatland farmer might give him," Wollerda said, "but it's all right with him as long as you treat him well."

Macurdy nodded. "I grew up a farmer, and I'll always have shit on my boots. So. Hog it is." He let go the halter and slapped the horse on the shoulder. It turned and trotted across the paddock to a rack of hay, then looked back at the two men.

"He's telling us something about relative importances," Wollerda said.

"Is it all right to thank you?" Macurdy asked. He felt closer to Wollerda than he'd ever expected to, and it was less the fact of the gift than what he'd learned about him in the giving: the man's ease and humor.

"Of course," Wollerda said. "It's the proper thing to do."

"Well then." Macurdy reached out, and gripping Wollerda's hand, shook it heartily. "Thanks a lot. I've got a feeling Hog and I are going to get along really well."

They climbed back over the paddock fence, Macurdy first, to round up their men. As Wollerda watched him go, he flexed his right hand, then felt it tentatively with his left, and wondered if Macurdy had any idea how strong he was.

* * *

When they were ready to leave, Macurdy asked another question. "Kithro told me the Kullvordi had shamans in the old days. Is that right?"

"Yes, they had shamans. Why do you ask?"

"After I got back from the Tuliptree, my guide told folks what happened there—what he knew of it. And of course, they already knew I start fires with magic, and my teeth are growing back. Now they talk about me as a shaman/warrior."

"I'm not surprised. What are you getting at?"

"You don't happen to have a shaman in your ancestry, do you?"

The question introverted Wollerda for a moment. "My great grandfather was the last chief of the eastern Kullvordi," he answered, "and his mother was the daughter of the greatest shaman they'd ever had. But the blood was lost by the time I came along, or thinned beyond all virtue." He cocked an eyebrow. "Why do you ask?"

Macurdy shrugged. "Till Varia worked with me," he said, "I didn't know I had the talent. And even a little helps."

Wollerda grunted. "You'll have to be shaman enough for both of us," he said. "I've never shown the slightest talent."

Then grinning, he put out his hand. They shook and parted, Wollerda thinking he should say something to Macurdy about his handshakes. The man would injure someone, someday.

* * *

On his ride back to camp, the afternoon felt more like mid-October than early September, lacking only haze and the smell of autumn leaves. As he rode, Macurdy mulled over things he hadn't adequately considered before. Most particularly Sarkia's policy of marrying kings to Sisters. With any luck at all, Wollerda would replace Gurtho, and Wollerda was eligible, a widower.

Varia had said it was difficult to spell most people against their will, if they suspected what you were up to. It was also difficult, she'd said, to get someone to do something strongly against their principles, even when they'd been spelled.

It seemed to him Pavo Wollerda was not someone who'd be spelled easily, but if he married a Sister, could Sarkia manipulate him through her?

Varia had said the person with significant talent was hard to spell without willing cooperation; if their talent had been trained, it was pretty much impossible. He'd asked her then why she'd been able to spell him, that first night. Her reply was; she hadn't. His will, his self determination, had been unimpaired. She'd gone to him leaving her body behind, and even though he'd been untrained, his talent had helped him see her spirit, or actually the image it projected. And because he knew her so well, instead of being frightened, and rejecting her, he'd accepted. Later, when she'd spelled him to help his training—spells not so different from hypnosis—she'd had his cooperation.

So. Say Wollerda married Liiset. Beautiful intelligent Liiset, who could no doubt turn on the sex appeal. Turn it on and back it up. How much could she influence Wollerda to do things against his own interest, and that of the Kullvordi or Tekalos?

A man was always being influenced by people around him: wife, friends—enemies as far as that was concerned. The real question was, if Wollerda married Liiset or some other Sister, would she be able to spell him? Wollerda's aura said he had significant talent, but it was untrained. And like himself at first, resisted it.

He decided when he got back to his tent, he'd take a quill, inkwell, and paper, and reconstruct, as best as he could, what Varia and Arbel had done to free and train his talent. Maybe he could free up Wollerda's, maybe even to the point of seeing auras clearly and consciously.

Chapter 32: Coronation

Once she had a covert agreement with them, Macurdy and Wollerda were astonished at how quickly Sarkia moved—quickly if not subtly.

But if her moves were quick, they'd been well prepared. Gurtho assumed he had a representative at the negotiations—Queen Idri. He'd already signed a secret alliance with the Sisterhood, and had appointed her his representative at what he considered three-cornered negotiations between himself, the Sisterhood, and the rebels. His understanding was the Sisterhood would use his authority, and their influence and presumed sorceries, to get an agreement that would end the rebellion. An agreement giving the Kullvordi virtual autonomy.

Then, when the time came to name and dedicate the triplets Idri was pregnant with, he'd proclaim and supply a day and night of festivities throughout Tekalos. He already had the brewing underway. Idri was to provide a poison with which to decimate the Kullvordi during the feasting, a delayed action poison undetectable in ale. The night of death would be followed by quickly hunting down any rebel officers surviving.

Meanwhile, as negotiations proceeded, he found an opportunity to have his existing sons and daughter meet with an unfortunate boating accident in which all three died, along with their mother. Whom Gurtho had divorced and set aside but not allowed to leave, because she was also his boughten property, his slave. This quadruple murder, he considered, removed all complications to the succession.

On the day after the cremation of his children and exwife,

however, Gurtho was found dead, poisoned. And because his queen-widow was away negotiating, there'd be problems in blaming her. She hurried home the next day, took the throne as regent, and turned management over to the Chief Minister, whom she'd earlier seduced. Then, before returning to the negotiations, she had Gurtho's valet poisoned. With his body was what seemed to be a suicide letter, in which he confessed to having poisoned his master out of love for the drowned exqueen.

The Council had intended to appoint their own regent. Their legal basis was weak, but that wasn't why they held back. They'd gotten to the palace before Idri, only to find her guard and Tiger companies in command. They then called on the commander of the royal cohort to take action, but he declined to act. And not simply out of caution; the queen had already seduced him thoroughly.

The Council had little choice but to accept her regency. Perhaps things would turn out all right.

* * *

The formal agreement with the rebels, signed by Idri as Queen Regent of Tekalos, and by Generals Wollerda and Macurdy for the eastern and western Kullvordi, had five main parts: (1) The hostilities were declared over. (2) The Kullvordi were granted tribal autonomy within the kingdom of Tekalos—with Pavo Wollerda as King. (3) Four Estates were now recognized, with their rights and property guaranteed. They were: the nobility; the yeomanry; the merchants and artisans; and the free laborers. (4) The Royal Council, known now as the Royal Assembly, was enlarged to include delegates from the new Estates. And (5), formulas and limits were established for taxation, with the exception of special war taxes.

The nobility wasn't thrilled with it, nor were the merchants, as previously theirs had been the only Estates with legal standing. But on the other hand, the rebellion and domestic uprisings were ended, and the future offered possible prosperity.

At the signing ceremony, in the Great Square of Teklapori, the honor guard consisted of a company of the royal cohort, and one from Wollerda's 1st Cohort, while in the saddle nearby sat a company of the Kullvordi 2nd Light Cavalry, known previously as Macurdy's Rebels. The Queen Regent's guard and Tiger companies were discreetly absent.

Macurdy wore well-fitting hillsmen's clothes of the best quality wadmal. They were much the same as flatland peasants wore, with the addition of leather sewn on the seat and the inside of thighs and knees to protect the breeches from wear while riding. Wore them as the openly stated symbol of the victory of both peoples.

That same afternoon, in a more elaborate and ornate ceremony, Queen Idri gracefully placed the crown of Tekalos on the head of Pavo Wollerda, who then spoke about a prosperous future. Afterward the newly enfranchised yeomen, artisans, and free laborers paraded cheering through the streets.

That evening the people drank the new king's beer, ate his beef and corn, and danced and caroused through the night. This time cheering the king himself, though no doubt some felt skeptical. The last Macurdy saw of Melody and Jeremid, about midnight, they were headed together for the palace where each had a room. He had no doubt they'd share one of them, and allowed himself to wish wistfully it was he who was hurrying off with her. He ended up drinking whiskey, and caught himself very nearly going to bed with a merchant's pretty and ambitious daughter.

He awoke next morning with his first hangover, mild but unpleasant, which along with his near seduction, he considered a lesson on drinking.

* * *

The next day, Sarkia left for the Cloister with her Tigers and guardsmen, taking Idri with her. And a copy of a previously drafted treaty of alliance that had been signed by King Pavo that morning as his first official act. Liiset stayed at Teklapori as Sarkia's ambassadrix. Macurdy had no doubt she'd been ordered to seduce Wollerda and become his bride, and said as much to the new king. Who grinned as if that was all right with him.

Macurdy was scheduled to leave Teklapori on a special mission for the Alliance, but earlier he'd had several evenings to work on activating his friend's latent psionic talent. The question, he told himself, was what, if anything, he'd accomplished.

* * *

Meanwhile, he, Wollerda and Liiset had sat down together one evening and designed new uniforms for the army. It would take time of course, to provide them. Officers would have theirs first, from the top down, and the uniforms of noncoms and men were already relatively simple and practical. The officers' looked rather like that of the commander of Sarkia's guard company, with the addition of the "Teklan Bear" on shoulder patches, the bear being the symbol of Teklan royalty and the kingdom. Also, for generals, the new dress uniform included a silver-plated cuirass and helmet, decorated and polished.

* * *

A week after Wollerda's crowning, a company of the 2nd Light Cavalry, wearing new uniforms, rode off westward down the Valley Highway, with General Macurdy and Majors Jeremid and Melody. Macurdy bore credentials from both Wollerda and the Dynast, as their joint envoy to the courts of Miskmehr and Kormehr, and to the Chief of Oz, authorizing him to negotiate an agreement of alliance with each of them.

It was the first mission in what would be the busiest fall, winter, and spring of Macurdy's life.

Chapter 33: An Introspective Morning at the Zoo

The Emperor's Animal Park had a foot of wet granular snow on the ground, but the morning was calm and sunny, and before noon already somewhat above freezing. A trickle of citizens strolled through the gate, many of them couples with one or more children hopping ahead.

One couple entered the park hand in hand. The woman was more warmly dressed than most, to humor her husband; with her talent, she'd have been comfortable with no coat at all. But she was pregnant, and he'd never been a father before.

Besides, she'd reasoned, *it's best not to draw attention.* Her husband had serious enemies, and among all of Duinarog's nearly sixty thousand people, there'd hardly be a hundred redheads other than herself. So she wore a fur cap well down over her ears.

There was no map on display, nor any directional signs. One simply walked the path until the large loop was completed; then you'd seen it all. But Cyncaidh had been there before, and knew what he wanted to show her first, so he turned left; that would take them first past animals of other regions. Briefly they stood watching the small herd of pronghorn, Cyncaidh telling her briefly about them, for he'd read the Animal Park booklet years earlier, and as a boy, other books on animals, and had excellent recall. Varia found the pronghorns uninteresting. It seemed to her that running, they'd be beautiful, but here they simply stood in the sun chewing their cuds, their auras reflecting placid contentment.

Beyond the pronghorns were wapiti. The bulls had shed

their antlers, but a cast-off pair had been mounted on a post, their spread approaching five feet. She thought she'd like to see wapiti in the wild someday, but didn't expect to. Next they came to the plains bison, with Cyncaidh describing the hunting tactics of the nomads. They sounded to Varia rather like descriptions she'd read of the Plains Indians on Farside. How marvelous it would be, she thought, to ride with them.

Next were the much larger long-horned bison. This was an animal of the near-arctic, with its broad mosaic of tundra, stunted forest, and bogs. These animals truly impressed her. One old bull had horns as wide as a man's outspread arms, and at the hump it stood as tall as Raien. She guessed its weight at two tons—more than Will's team of big Belgians, the gelding and mare combined. According to Raien, these animals didn't form great herds, but wandered in bands of two or three dozen, grazing on grasses and sedges, browsing the low shrubs. She wondered how they'd been brought here. As calves, she decided.

She also wondered what could possibly prey on them—and then found out, for they came next to the lions. She'd seen lions before, the African *Panthera leo*, when she and Will visited the zoo in Indianapolis. And clearly these *were* lions, though their winter fur—white tinged faintly with pink—was thicker than the African, and the males wore ruffs instead of manes. She hadn't imagined lions existing on this continent. And *what* lions, the males much larger than the African. The Cloister school hadn't mentioned lions of any sort, while on Farside, the long-extinct American lion, *Panthera atrox*, she'd never heard of.

Probably the Cloister's teachers hadn't known of lions, she told herself. But surely someone there had known of Duinarog, and the Northern, Middle, and Imperial Seas, yet they hadn't been mentioned either. At the Cloister, the world virtually ended at the Big River. The Marches, and the Western and Eastern Empires which lay north of them, were spoken of only in political terms. It occurred to her Sarkia didn't want her people to know wonder or feel curiosity, and certainly not to be honestly informed. Everything was seen in terms of her own explanations, ambitions, and hatreds.

The dire wolves were next, conspicuously larger than timber wolves, and more strongly built. They hunted the plains bison, Raien told her. After the dire wolves they saw tundra caribou, and shaggy musk oxen no larger than ponies. Next were animals from nearer climes. Moose: tall, gangling, and nearly black. She'd seen them wild near Aaerodh Manor; they'd looked better there. In the next enclosure were timber wolves, looking lazy and bored, which was hardly surprising. She liked them better than she had the dire wolves; they seemed less—less dire.

And ah! Northern jaguars, particularly beautiful in their winter coats. Physically they were much less impressive than the lions—two hundred pounds she guessed, three at most—but regal, even here in the zoo. It was partly their auras. She smiled at Raien, whom she knew had a special love for these cats. And wished they were still at Aaerodh Manor, where she would have learned to run on skis, and they'd have gone stalking together. How fulfilling it would be to see these wonderful ice-blue creatures crossing a frozen lake, or padding along some moose trail in a cedar swamp. Now the odds seemed poor she ever would. They planned to go back for a few weeks each summer, circumstances permitting, but she didn't expect to live there year-round, ever. For being the Emperor's Chief Counselor meant he'd probably be chosen Emperor when Paedrigh declined.

Raien didn't covet the throne for itself, but for what he could do as Emperor: Continue and perhaps even complete the reforms and other projects he and Paedrigh had plotted and planned, back when Paedrigh had been Chief Counselor, and Raien his military adviser. Notably the end of ducal armies large enough to threaten the imperial peace; the end of slavery; and the beginnings of peace with the rest of the continent.

All to be accomplished in the face of factionalized and discordant politics, as reflected in the Imperial Council.

Braighn IV had reformed the slave laws, and Paedrigh had modified them further, but slaves were still subject to abuses, particularly the girls and women. Abuses that degraded the abusers as well, Raien had told her—nobles and gentry who took advantage of their position, and justified it by insisting slaves had no souls.

There was a faction, an important political party, based on the concept the ylver had a natural right to rule and dominate "humans," whom they looked at as an only quasi-sapient species. The same party upheld fiercely the rights of slaveholders, though many slaves were descended from ylvin prisoners of ducal wars long past. Almost always they were conspicuously only part ylvin. It had become awkward to justify ylvin slaves, thus they'd been deliberately crossbred with human slaves. The more they looked like ordinary humans, the easier it was to rationalize their slavery.

Raien had pointed out what the books she'd read had slighted—that there were few if any ylver without some non-ylvin ancestry. To speak of half-ylver was a simplification. A half-ylf was someone who had enough human ancestry—especially recent human ancestry—that it showed plainly. The race of ylver, he said, was a blend, with a preponderance of ylvin ancestry.

Legend had it there'd been mixing even before the ylver came here across the Eastern Ocean. For example, red hair among ylver was supposed to be a sign of ancient mixing with the mythical *Voitusotar*, who were said to live in a land of fog and ice and sorcery. Mothers and nurses still sometimes told children the Voitusotar would get them if they weren't good, though such threats were frowned on these days. Interestingly, red hair tended generally to be admired, perhaps because the Voitusotar had been feared. Though that admiration didn't extend to those of the Sisterhood.

While Varia let her mind wander, they'd passed the lesser cats—bobcat and lynx—the foxes, and the gracefully tireless mustelines. Raien, aware of her preoccupation, had discontinued his monologues on wildlife. Finally the loop took them past paddocks with farm animals, which after twenty years of farm life, hardly excited Varia. At the end they each put a gold piece in the donations box, and she squeezed her husband's hand affectionately. He was more than just an idealist with intelligence, talent, will and political power. He was a good and decent person.

And he'd be an excellent father, as he was a husband and

lover.

PART 5: *War*

Chapter 34: Invasion

There was still enough twilight Melody could see the camps spread around her, the armies of five kingdoms and one tribe, their cook fires dying, their tents low shadowed humps. No doubt some of their men were already asleep.

They'd get little enough of it this night.

Late Five-Month had advantages and disadvantages for invasion. Grazing was good, and they had the whole summer ahead of them, if need be. On the other hand, the season was subject to thunderstorms, and the nights were short. And tonight they had much to do between nightfall and dawn, especially between nightfall and moonrise.

She recognized the Indrossan command tent by the torches lashed to spears thrust in the ground beside its entrance. And as she approached, by its being guarded. She dismounted in front of it, handed the reins to her orderly, and loud and clear, identified herself to the guards as Marshal Macurdy's aide, then told them to take her to their commander.

And waited. Despite her position, and her bright new colonel's insignia, they stared back insolently, showing no sign of obeying. So she drew her saber, and before either man realized what she had in mind, held its point to the belly of the nearest.

"You son of a bitch! Did you hear what I said? How do you want it? Quick and bloody, here and now? Or at a rope's end tomorrow, pulled up to strangle from a branch after a drumhead court?"

The man backed away into the entrance, and she followed, keeping her blade at his belly while her aide, a Kullvordi, followed with his own saber, covering her back. When she was inside, she shouted the Indrossan general's name. "Eldersov! I have orders for you from Marshal Macurdy!"

It wasn't entirely dark inside. She could see a short corridor through the tent, with rooms on each side set off by curtains. Lamplight filtered through two of them, and a hand brushed one aside. "General!" the guard squawked. "She drew her sword on me and forced her way in!"

"You miserable get of a troll and a sow!" Melody snapped, "An insult to me is an insult to the marshal!" Her glance shifted to the general. "I'm Marshal Macurdy's aide. I stopped at the entrance, showed them my baton of authority, and told them I had orders to deliver to you from the marshal. They stood there and sneered."

His grunt dripped scorn. "You're a woman. We don't take orders from women here."

"They're not my orders, they're Marshal Macurdy's. Do you refuse them? When I carry a message from the marshal, I speak with his voice."

"We take no one's orders from a woman."

Abruptly her sword tip moved from the guard to the general. "You just signed your death warrant, general. Unless you reconsider." Even while she said it, she knew he wouldn't, which it seemed to her was just as well. Otherwise he'd be a source of trouble and danger throughout the campaign. "No? Where's your second in command?"

Another curtain had been pushed aside; now a man stepped out. "I'm Colonel Lidsok."

"Colonel, you are now in command of the Indrossan Army. General Eldersov is under arrest. I'm taking him to the marshal's headquarters for trial."

With his curtain open, enough light shone into the corridor that the colonel could see the woman's teeth. Lidsok hesitated, unsure. Her wrist twitched and the sword tip bit, not deeply, slicing Eldersov's skin. "Sergeant at arms!" he shrieked, "arrest these intruders!"

Shit! she thought, and thrust hard with her sword, her wrist half turning. *What lousy timing.* For just a moment, Eldersov stared down at his belly while his life's blood poured from his severed aorta into his abdominal cavity. Then his knees buckled, and he pitched forward dead, Melody stepping aside. While she'd talked, another man had emerged from a room toward the rear, saber in fist. The sergeant at arms, she decided, and ignored him. "Colonel," she said, "do you reject Marshal Macurdy's orders?"

Again Lidsok hesitated, more from not knowing how to address this bloody madwoman than anything else. Ma'am? Sir? He settled on rank. "No, Colonel," he said. "I do not reject them."

"Did you hear Eldersov refuse Marshal Macurdy's orders? And order the marshal's aide arrested?"

"Yes, Colonel. I heard him do both those things."

"Good. I suggest you tell your sergeant at arms to drag the carrion out of here and have it tied across a horse. I'll stop on my way back to the marshal's headquarters, and take it with me. Eldersov's no loss. If a general refuses his commander's orders, particularly in war, God knows how much disaster and death he'll bring on people, his and his allies. Now, let's get down to business. You'll be crossing the river tonight, and I've got orders for four more armies to deliver within the hour."

Lidsok looked at the sergeant at arms. "You heard the marshal's aide. Drag the body out."

Reluctantly the sergeant at arms sheathed his saber, came over to his late general, took him under the arms, and began dragging him toward the tent's back entrance. Melody became aware the guard she'd followed in still stood there.

She spoke softly, enunciating. "Do you have a post, soldier?" she asked.

He looked to his colonel, then back at Melody. "Uh, yessir."

"Good. Return to it. And keep your mouth shut. I've got a good memory for faces."

The man sidled away, then turned out through the entrance.

"Colonel, I presume you know your loading area and boats?"

"Yes, Colonel. I'm our embarkation commander."

"Good. Have your troops strike and pack their tents as drilled, and leave them. In two hours—two hours—your army will be on the shore, ready to go. Their gear will follow in the morning. Any problem with that? Tell me if there is."

"None whatever, Colonel. And Colonel?"

"Yes?"

"In my view, General Eldersov was not fit to command, and most of his officers feel the same. But he was a crony of the king's; trouble may grow from this."

"Thank you, Colonel. At your first opportunity you'll write to your king, telling him just what happened here. That's an order, in the interest of the alliance. Perhaps his new wife will help him see reason."

With her aide she left the tent then, mounted her horse and rode away in the twilight, leaving two awed guards staring after her.

* * *

Terel Kithro—Major Kithro—was the "crossing marshal," responsible for coordinating the embarkation of the various armies. Not the easiest of jobs. Significant mental lapses among key officers could cause chaos.

The moon wouldn't rise till after midnight, and the Milky Way produced light enough to see only vaguely his immediate surroundings. Torches and bonfires had been forbidden along the river, and loud talk, because sound carries well over water, and the enemy was less than a mile away on the other shore.

But each embarkation commander and each cohort commander was marked by a loose white cap or wrapping over whatever helmet or other headgear he had on. Also, Kithro had a head for details, quick intelligence, and a responsive memory. He walked briskly along the shore, knowing every motley concentration of small boats, and the cohorts and companies assigned to them. He stopped to speak briefly with each senior commander.

Each cohort commander would ride its lead boat, and Kithro

reminded each of them the bridgehead commander, in the first boat of all, might elect to change course while crossing. The cohort flotillas needed to follow each other closely enough they would see and duplicate any course change, upstream or down. The bridgehead commander, General Jeremid, had already told them this, not an hour earlier, but it was well to repeat it.

There were compelling reasons only cohort commanders were being told, and in a murmur. Venders of various sorts had been mixing with the soldiers as the camp filled up, and surely there were spies among them. Thus the crossing plan involved one deceit underlying another, and even now, only four men knew all of it, Kithro one of them. As things progressed, of course, the enemy commander would figure it out, more or less, but the later, the better.

Earlier, Kithro had seen a fire lit on a small hill upstream a bit, probably some spy's signal, though what the ylvin commander made of it, there was no telling. A spy was unlikely to have a boat available to take word to him, unless he'd managed to stash one in a shed somewhere. But even so, he'd have to launch it above or below the fleet.

Presumably the ylvin general already knew three more armies were still enroute a day or two away, marching and riding toward the staging area. And hopefully hadn't expected a crossing until all the southern armies were on hand.

Along the south shore, all but the smallest boats had been commandeered for many miles in both directions, including its southern tributaries. Raiders had snatched barges and ferries even from the north shore, to help transport the cavalry. The miscellaneous smaller boats would carry infantry.

Kithro passed the last of the small boats, and came to the wharves along which the barges now were tied, packed tightly with horses and warriors—the Kormehri cavalry cohort. The Kormehri were the only troops with whom Kithro felt uncomfortable. Their peculiar sense of honor had turned bitter and cruel after the terrible events at Ferny Cove, and their smoldering vengefulness gave off a stink of violence. Meanwhile they waited grimly for the bridgehead commander to lead off.

Jeremid and two companies of Kullvordi cavalry would cross on ferries. As Kithro came up to them, he saw they too had already loaded, as crowded as the Kormehri. Jeremid would be waiting, no doubt impatiently, for word things were ready.

Jeremid's ferry was the farthest downstream, tied sternon to the wharf in a sort of slip, and held against the current by a bow line. On her stern, two raised platforms flanked the ramp, one for the steersman, one for the bosun. Jeremid, on the bosun's platform, watched Kithro clomp up the ramp onto the boat. Its oarsmen half sat on tall seats, oars upright.

He could feel Jeremid's glower, and imagined the nervous stress he felt. "Everything's fine," Kithro murmured. "Pull out whenever you want; just let me off first. Us old crocks are too brittle for fighting."

It had been the right thing to say; he could feel Jeremid lighten, and heard him chuckle. "All right, old crock, get off and we'll get started. I'll see you after the war."

Let us hope, Kithro told himself. When he was on the wharf, the bosun and his helper raised the loading ramp with a windlass, the rattling of its well-greased chain a signal. A moment later he heard Jeremid speak quietly to the bosun, who called softly, "Oars in the water and give her slack." Kithro saw the oars lower, felt the wharf bumped by the stern. The dockers cast off the lines. Quietly the bosun grunted "stroke"; there'd be no drum beat to regulate the rowing tonight. The oarsmen pulled and the boat drew away, sluggishly as if dragging bottom. Meanwhile a courier, who'd been waiting for an hour, nudged his horse's barrel and trotted away toward camp, to inform Macurdy the crossing had begun.

Now too, Kithro knew, a sleek, carvel-built river cutter would be pulling out, Jesker in command, with five similar cutters following closely. Each held Kullvordi brawlers, men selected for their fighting attitudes, three of them bending strong backs to the oars, while a half dozen more sat with spears and axes. Those in Jesker's boat were to cut loose any craft tied at the landing site, freeing the docks for the troop carriers. The men in the other cutters would defend the axmen and their work, and hold the wharves if need be.

Kithro watched the second ferry pull away from the next dock upstream, and beyond that another, and another. First the ferries, then the barges moved out into the current, disappearing into the night. When the last barge pulled out, the small boats would follow.

But not with all the men; there weren't nearly enough boats for that. The rest stood in ranks in camp. In a few minutes, Macurdy's courier would reach headquarters, and Macurdy would speed march the remaining troops five miles downstream to the Inderstown docks—another part of his fabric of deceit.

* * *

Jeremid's gaze was not ahead toward the unseen north shore, but back toward the south shore. When it was only a vaguely darker darkness, he began to count slowly. At thirty, he spoke to the bosun. "Turn downstream and hold course near the middle, until I tell you otherwise. I don't want us seen from either shore." *Not that some cat-eyed ylf can't see us if he's watching. But it can make him uncertain; make him stop and puzzle.*

The bosun had been prepared for a change in course, but this? "Yes, General," he answered, and ordered the steersman, who pulled hard on the steering oar, turning them sharply left. The oarsmen continued to dip and pull their long oars, despite the break in the bosun's soft and rhythmic chant of "Stroke." With the current, they were making good speed. Upstream there was no light yet from the moonrise to come, and downstream Jeremid still couldn't see the guide torches that should have been lit at dusk. Had better have been, or this operation could run into serious trouble. Though if it came down to it, they'd make it work somehow.

Briefly he turned his attention to what he thought of as the troop deck. Between the oarsmen's narrow halfdecks, with their low protective railings, the cargo deck was packed with horses, each with its rider standing by its head, one hand gripping the bridle while the other stroked the animal's long nose, or its neck. The horses were another source of possible trouble when they docked.

Shortly Jeremid saw a row of torches ahead on the south shore, and spoke to the bosun. "Steer for the Parnston docks. The rest of the army is marching to Inderstown; they'll cross to Parnston from there." The order drew an "ah" of understanding, and the bosun ordered the steersman, who pushed on the steering oar, angling them right. By starlight, Jeremid could make out the next two ferries following, could even hear a low voice calling an order on the nearest—nearer than he liked.

The north shore became more distinct, until at about sixty yards, the bosun gave another order and the steersman turned parallel to it. A minute later, Jeremid made out the Parnston barge docks ahead. Now if Jesker had done his job...He had: the barge and ferry docks were clear. The bosun gave more orders, sharply now. The steersman turned them sharply. Oars were raised or backed water, and for long seconds Jeremid forgot to breathe. The oars dipped again, stroked once, then backed strongly; the ferry dragged bottom slightly, and bumped the wharf just enough to throw Jeremid against the bosun's rail. Men jumped onto the wharf with lines, while the portside oarsmen dug blades into the muddy bottom, holding the ferry in place till the lines were secured. Then the bosun ordered the forward ramp lowered.

Several horses had fallen when the ferry bumped the wharf, but they all got up again; there'd been no broken legs. Jeremid was the first to lead his gelding up the ramp, at the same time aware of shouts and swearing from other ferries docking without benefit of longshoremen. He scowled; what he didn't need was wrecks, horses with broken legs, or boats colliding, perhaps dumping their troops into the current.

Ashore, his men stood by their horses. Jesker's advance landing party stood watching; if it had been in a fight, there was no sign of it. They should have a beacon fire ready for lighting. "Jesker!" Jeremid called.

"Here, sir!"

"Light it off!"

"Yes, sir!"

If Macurdy were here, the Ozman thought, *he'd have it in flames with a gesture.* He looked downstream. It was the barges and the crazy Kormehri he needed to see to now.

* * *

Subcolonel Caill Cearnigh was thoroughly at home in the saddle. He'd been a horseman since childhood, and had passed the midpoint of the century he expected to live. As for riding by night—while his night vision wasn't the best, it was a lot better than any of the Rude Landers', he had no doubt. Though the advantage was less with the cupped, newly risen moon throwing its light across the land.

Whoever the southern commander was, he'd shown himself both clever, and capable of complex staging and coordination. But simple arithmetic made it clear the numbers the man could have landed so soon, half-trained humans that they were, couldn't begin to hold a landing zone against ylvin cavalry. Certainly not without trenches, ramparts, and troll brambles, and they'd had no time even to begin making them.

Cearnigh had elected to lead his seven companies down the road that paralleled the river. It was quicker and safer, for nearer the river, the land was public pastures. Which had rail fences along jurisdictional lines, and woodchuck and gopher holes a horse could break a leg in.

At their easy trot, his companies should be there in another quarter hour. And then…He knew the terrain around Parnston. The southerners had probably taken positions along the wooded west bank of the Sweet Gum River, but it was neither broad nor deep, and the banks were low.

"Colonel!" It was his sergeant major. "Do you hear them?"

Cearnigh shook off his musings, and listening, heard a faint rumble of hoofbeats.

"It sounds as if they've sent out cavalry, Colonel."

Where in hell were they? The sound wasn't from up the road. Ahead and to the left, that was it, cut off from view by a low rounding of land. And not far away.

"They must hear us, Colonel, if we hear them." The sergeant major sounded concerned.

Cearnigh had overlooked that. "Obviously, Sergeant," he said, and called an order to his trumpeter. The instrument's crystal notes brought the column to a halt. Another order turned the westward-bound column into three ranks facing south. The next sent them off the road, rank by rank, again at an easy trot, shields raised, spears at the ready. They'd gone only a short way when the southern cavalry topped the rise about three hundred yards ahead. A single weird cry, a warbling epiglottal shrilling uncanny in the night, triggered a wild clamor, and the invaders spurred their mounts into a canter, charging downhill at the ylver.

For just a moment, Cearnigh felt dismay tinged with panic. Then he barked a command. Trumpets belled, and his troopers spurred their horses, but even on such a mild slope, they had no momentum when the barbarians crashed into them. A smashing blow pierced Cearnigh's shield, wrenched his arm and drove him from the saddle. Somehow he got to his feet without being trampled, aware his arm was useless, the shoulder dislocated or separated. As he drew his saber, a riderless horse knocked him down. He felt an instant of shock as a forehoof came down on his belly, then a hind hoof crushed his rib cage.

* * *

The trumpeter saw his colonel unseated, then the ranks passed through each other, and somehow he was still in his saddle, untouched by any enemy. As a trumpeter, his only weapon was his saber. He lacked even a shield, and as soon as they'd passed through, the enemy wheeled, this time closing with drawn steel. The wild war cry had ceased, replaced by shouts of "FERNY COVE! FERNY COVE!" The air was thick with them, and with impacts, grunts, inarticulate cries, the screams of horses. An enemy singled him out and struck at him. He took the blow on his saber, a blow of more force than he would have imagined, almost paralyzing his arm. Then they'd passed again.

Two things occurred to him at once: The cohort must flee— it was that or be butchered—and no one was in charge. With his left hand he raised his trumpet, and unordered blew retreat, then spurred his horse back toward the road.

But there was no safety in flight. Shouts of "FERNY COVE! FERNY COVE!" pursued him closely. Something—a horse's shoulder—struck his mount from behind, throwing it off stride, and he turned to his left to see the horse that had done it, its rider's face a glimpsed grimace. Then someone on the other side struck his thigh with a saber. He felt and heard his own scream, then the ground slammed him, and he bounced and rolled. For a moment, perhaps a minute, he lay stunned. At least a minute, for when he regained his wits somewhat, the sound of hooves was gone.

And he hadn't been trampled! He reached, felt his bloody thigh. The man who'd struck him had been right handed, had had to swivel in the saddle as he'd passed, and the blow had lacked force. Even so, he couldn't stand, but lay shocked, mentally and physically.

What manner of enemy were these, so full of rage and deadly purpose? Shouting "Ferny Cove" as they rode in pursuit. Who had looked at him with such hatred? Kormehri, obviously.

* * *

Colonel Morghild inspected his smashed camp, his shattered companies. As force commander, he'd sent two companies of his own cohort along with Cearnigh's. Holding back three, along with the militia cohorts. Then the Rude Landers had come, and most of the militia had scattered without fighting. His own men had fought of course, fought and fallen. And the enemy, after trampling the camp, had whirled back westward.

Fragments of Cearnigh's companies had ridden, walked, or been helped back to camp, some still straggling in after sunup. Altogether, of more than 1,100 imperial officers and men, 362 were known to be fit for duty, and 334 others reported wounded and unfit. Which left some 400 killed or missing. Morale too had been smashed, and would take time to rebuild.

As far as the militia was concerned, if he had his way, they could stay wherever they'd scattered to. But having one's way wasn't part of military service, so he would round them up, all he could, eat the ass out of their officers, and see what could be made of them.

As for the Rude Landers, they'd been ferrying men across since midnight. Apparently they had no intention of fortifying their landing zone; attack was their strategy.

And "Ferny Cove!" their rallying cry. Their attackers had almost surely been Kormehri. Quaie's atrocities against the Sisterhood had received most of the publicity, perhaps properly so, but it was well known Quaie had slaughtered the Kormehri companies he'd overrun, taking no prisoners and butchering the wounded.

And now, Morghild told himself, *we have our reward. Too bad Quaie isn't here so they can pin it on him in person, with a Kormehri saber.*

Chapter 35: Duinarog

The jingling persisted, plucking at a corner of his dream until his wife laid a hand on his shoulder. "Raien," she said, "Talrie's ringing."

The Cyncaidh pushed himself upright, groaning. The angle of sunlight through the gap in the curtains told him it wasn't nearly seven yet; why would Talrie be waking him this early? He swung his legs out of bed. "What is it?" he called.

"Your lordship, I have an urgent message for you from the palace. You're wanted there for an eight o'clock meeting. The courier is in the foyer, awaiting your acknowledgement."

Cyncaidh grunted, and turned to his wife. "I hope this doesn't mean what it might," he muttered, then raised his voice again. "Just a moment."

At the door, his steward handed him an envelope, its wax seal pressed with the emperor's signet. "Thank you, Talrie," he said, and went to his dressing table, where his penknife lay in its sheath. Slitting the envelope, he withdrew the paper folded inside, scanned it, then turned soberly to where Talrie stood discreetly outside the door. "Tell the courier I'll be there in good time," he called, "and have our horses ready by seven."

Varia had already disappeared into her bathroom. Cyncaidh went to his, and instead of drawing a bath, knelt in his tub, drew a pitcher of cold water, and poured it over his head, sputtering and gasping. Then he drew warm water, and washed. Shaving wasn't necessary. It was a rare ylf who grew facial hair below the eyebrows; they were likelier to be hairless entirely.

When both had dressed, they went together to their private

dining nook overlooking the Imperial River, and the splendid park below their bluff. The morning was cool, and the broad balcony doors only slightly ajar, just enough to let in birdsong from the trees below. Morning sunlight slanted through the numerous panes, and Talrie had adjusted a shade wing so it wouldn't shine in her ladyship's eyes.

While waiting for their omelettes and toast, they sipped the almost obligatory sassafras tea with honey. Varia reread the short message, then looked up, frowning.

"What can she possibly hope to accomplish? I'd assumed the alliance was a ploy, a step in some long-term plan for political union. But to actually invade?" She shook her head. "Perhaps Ferny Cove pushed her over the edge."

"Perhaps it started as a ploy," Cyncaidh suggested, "and got out of control. At any rate she's playing into my hands. And Quaie's as well."

Quaie. The Rude Lands alliance had already increased his influence. The man frightened her. The only time she'd met him, at a palace banquet, his eyes had done more than undress her. If she ever fell into his hands, it seemed to her her fate would be worse than the captured Sisters' at Ferny Cove; he'd keep her alive longer. For she was not only one of what he referred to in his circulars as "Sarkia's brood of witches"; she was Cyncaidh's wife.

Don't think like that! she told herself sharply. *It's not the sort of situation to create in your subjective world. It might start solidifying!*

Quaie's hatreds were extravagant and beyond understanding. He scorned humans; seemingly hated any of them not subject to ylvin authority. But most conspicuously he hated Sisters; they were his most cherished hatred, particularly since Ferny Cove. And he hated anyone who opposed him, notably her husband. Like most hatreds, Quaie's were no doubt rooted in fear, though of what, even A'duaill hadn't discerned.

In a sense, he seemed to disdain even the talent that marked his own race. A large majority of ylver lit fires without tinder or flint, protected themselves from insects by weaving repellent fields, speeded their own healing. Like strength, intelligence and beauty, talent varied between individuals; that was understood. But some, a small percentage, disapproved of or distrusted those whose talent went beyond their own. Which included most who ruled. These disapprovers weren't a political faction, but they saw in Quaie a kindred soul, and supported him.

Varia wondered what A'duaill might find if he were free to interrogate Quaie as he had her the summer before.

Her reverie was interrupted by a serving girl with their cart, and she became aware her husband had been watching her. He smiled ruefully. "Perhaps I shouldn't have mentioned Quaie," he said, and spread jam on a toasted muffin.

She smiled back, also ruefully. "It's odd," she said, "to think of you two having any common ground at all. I suppose Murdoth will be there this morning."

"He's sure to be."

"He's as bad as Quaie."

Cyncaidh chuckled. "Not really. But he's often thorny where Quaie would be oily."

Varia made a face. "Oily and venomous."

As she spread her toast, she deliberately turned her thoughts to Curtis. He'd no doubt left Illinois for Washington County, where his life would be ruled largely by weather and the other straightforward realities of farming. She'd cleared him for the long ylvin youth. What ill effects might that have on him now, without her? He'd probably remarry, then watch his wife and children age. No doubt he'd have to leave them eventually. Washington County had no place for a man forever twenty-five years old.

If it hadn't been for Idri...If it hadn't been for Idri, she wouldn't be here with Raien.

Cyncaidh didn't break in on her reveries again that morning. By her face as much as her aura, it was best to leave her with them.

* * *

The emperor's council room had one large oval table, around which sat the council's dozen members, none of whom

looked older than twenty-five, though at least one or two besides
the Emperor had passed eighty. There were also two recording
secretaries armed with piles of slender graphite crayons, and two
consultants, one of them Varia, for her knowledge of the Sisterhood.

The other was a Captain Docheri from Morghild's command, who'd worn out a series of post horses in four eighteen-
hour days of hard riding, to report. Since arriving last night, he'd
slept seven hours, then been wakened gray-faced and groggy, to
wash, dress, and eat before the meeting.

Cyncaidh read the report aloud to the Council. It was sobering, though it had less information than he'd expected. The
southern commander's strategy was described—the unexpectedly early crossing, the landing at Parnston instead of Cur-
ryville, and the forced march of units to Inderstown to complete
the crossing more quickly. It also described the smashing foray
of the Kormehri cavalry, identified with certainty by their uniforms and by questioning wounded prisoners. And by their war
cry, "Ferny Cove."

Varia's gaze switched to Lord Murdoth. He'd reddened angrily, his aura darkening and thickening. As if the Kormehri had
somehow wronged Quaie by hating him for his barbarities.

The number of imperial casualties were given, but those of
the March militia cohorts were only estimated, their troops having scattered badly.

Docheri then gave an oral report, and when he'd finished,
the emperor asked the first question: "How," he wondered, "did
we so drastically underestimate the southern alliance?"

In a sense the question was rhetorical. The evaluations had
been made in that room, by himself and this council. But Docheri
answered. "Your Majesty, we had no idea the allies would work
so well together. Or coordinate at all; there was no precedent
for it. Actually the alliance seemed somewhat of a joke, though
neither Colonel Morghild nor Colonel Cearnigh treated it as one.
But obviously its commander is an unexpectedly skilled leader
and military planner."

Murdoth snorted, his glance touching Varia on its way to the emperor. "The Sisterhood's to blame," he said. "They've married sorceresses to every ruler south of the river." He paused, glaring again at Varia as if adding mentally *and one north of it*. Then went on, "And controls them like marionettes; I have no doubt if the light were right, you could see the strings."

The speaker of the majority Empire Party, spoke next. "If it weren't for our ill-advised expedition to Kormehr, and the outrages at Ferny Cove, none of this would have…"

Murdoth interrupted angrily. "That vile Dynast has lived for more than two centuries, and has dreamed of our destruction the whole time. She—"

The emperor's light gavel struck the bell in front of him, its brittle clang cutting Murdoth off sharply. "Lord Murdoth, we have rules of courtesy here. Do not interrupt again." His gaze went to Varia. "Lady Cyncaidh, do you have any comments on the role of the Sisterhood in this?"

"Speculative comments, Your Majesty. The Dynast has always been strongly prejudiced against Your Empire, and taught us to fear and loathe it. But the Rape at Ferny Cove seems clearly to have changed her approach. Previously she'd had a treaty only with the Kormehri, and that only for the use of an area of land, and the protection of the Sisterhood within its boundaries. While giving the Kormehri unique rights in marketing the Sisterhood's products."

"May we suppose that the military commander is one of her people? Perhaps the commander of her guard forces?"

"It seems quite possible, Your Majesty."

At this, Captain Docheri raised his hand.

"Yes, Captain?"

"We know a bit about the commander's identity, Your Majesty. His name is Makurdi. He's said to be an Ozman, who somehow came to Tekalos and led a rebellion that overthrew the king there."

Macurdy! At the name, Cyncaidh's glance went to Varia, just for a moment. Her bright green gaze had snapped to the captain like a compass needle to a lump of magnetite.

"An Ozman," the emperor said thoughtfully. "The Ozmen

have a considerable military reputation."

He turned the discussion to how they might respond to the invasion. After consulting briefly during a break, the Empire Party, with its plurality in both the Council and the biennial Great Parliament, kept as close as it could to its isolationist tradition. Its position was that the militias and garrisons should carry the burden of defense, the March taking the major responsibility. The Throne Army should not be involved; the invaders couldn't possibly fight their way to the border of the empire. However, to reassure the Marches, a senior crown officer, perhaps Lord Cyncaidh, should coordinate the defense.

The A'conal Party—in these days the center party—went a long step further. Lord Finntagh was its official spokesman in the Council, to support the fiction of the Emperor's neutrality. Finntagh recommended the 1st Imperial Legion be sent south to the Elmintoss military reservation, ready to enter the Inner Marches if the invaders reached them.

Predictably, Murdoth proposed the ducal armies be imperialized, and march south with the Throne Army, to crush the invaders utterly so they could never come back.

When he'd sat down, Cyncaidh stood. "Who," he asked, "do you propose should lead that army?"

Murdoth glared, and after a moment answered, "If the decision was mine, I'd name General Quaie."

"And what disposition would you make of enemy prisoners?"

Murdoth's glare intensified, his face threatening to swell like a balloon. "I'd hold a slave sale," he said.

Cyncaidh nodded. "Would they be safe to keep around as slaves? In large numbers?"

"There'd be no large numbers."

"Ah. I suppose not, with Lord Quaie in command. And what would you recommend he do with his army, when he reached the Big River?"

Murdoth turned to the Emperor. "Your Majesty, I object to your chief counselor's insults!"

"Your objection is noted, but I fail to see an insult. Please answer. I'm interested."

Murdoth took a steadying breath. "He should do with it—whatever Your Majesty wishes."

"Thank you, Lord Murdoth. Lord Cyncaidh, what was your motive in asking?"

"General Quaie might be tempted to cross the river on his own determination, to punish the Rude Lands for their invasion."

Murdoth broke in. "General Quaie might very properly wish to. As I would. But he'd never make such a move without Your Majesty's authorization."

"Indeed he wouldn't. Because if I were to imperialize the ducal armies, which I would only do if my own forces were insufficient, I would not appoint General Quaie to their command. He is a skilled and proven military leader, but I have learned not to trust his judgment in victory." He paused, looking around the table. "Well. Gentlemen, I will not make any firm decisions without knowing more than we do now. Which we certainly will, quite soon. And while there are other matters we could discuss, there are none that can't wait. I am going to conclude this meeting."

He turned to Cyncaidh. "Chief Counselor, do you have any last words?"

"Only that I'd like to question Captain Docheri on details that may cast light on southern strengths and limitations."

"As you wish. Gentlemen, we'll meet here again tomorrow at nine. We may well have further information on the war by then; perhaps the invaders' initial success will have been reversed. Meanwhile, good day."

Chair legs scraped, feet shuffled, and the Council left. The Emperor watched the last of them out, then nodded Cyncaidh and the captain into his adjacent chamber, an intent Varia following. When they were seated, the emperor looked musingly at her before speaking. "Lady Cyncaidh, you seem to have heard something in Captain Docheri's testimony that I missed; something that seemingly your husband also caught. Something to do with the southern commander. Perhaps we should clear that up before questioning the captain on other matters."

"Thank you, Your Majesty. You are most considerate." She turned to Docheri. "Makurdi. It's certainly a strange name. Is it his given or his surname?"

"Your ladyship, that brings us to a somewhat less believable part of the story. He's said to be an escaped Ozian slave. And if that's true, he has no formal surname."

She gnawed a lip. "A slave. What brought an Ozian slave to Tekalos?"

"The stories our sources told are at second hand, or third or fourth, which makes them more difficult to accept. Some of them seem—quite fanciful. The important part is what we know for certain: he is formidable."

"Nonetheless, the stories may reflect elements of truth. And the Merchants Guild may be able to refer my husband to men who were in Tekalos during the rebellion or since. The more he knows, the better able he'll be to question them. I want you to tell us everything you've heard of this Makurdi, regardless of how unlikely it seems."

"Well, my lady," Docheri said, "the story is that although a slave, this Makurdi had somehow married one of the Sisterhood. And she'd been stolen from him, and he'd run away from his master to find her." The captain paused, as if to see if she'd had enough. She nodded him on. "Then somehow, with the help of dwarves he'd rescued from bandits—" the captain paused again, shrugging, as if to say that should give them some idea of how far-fetched the stories were "—with the help of dwarves, he freed a number of rebels held prisoner in the king's very courtyard, standing off and killing a number of king's men singlehandedly while they escaped. Then, supposedly, he got away and fled into the mountains, where he met a great boar and ensorceled it to carry him on its back. That's another thing: he's said to be a magician. He then gathered together an army of Kullvordi." Docheri shrugged. "Supposedly his lieutenant is a beautiful Ozian spear maiden who followed him out of love, but he's spurned her because he cannot love any woman but his lost wife, who'd cast a spell on him."

He spread his hands apologetically. "And that seems to be

all of it. Oh! Except that he has two rows of teeth, all the way around!" The captain showed his own in an almost smile.

The emperor had watched Docheri's aura for any sign he was making it up, in whole or in part. Seemingly he was being entirely honest.

Cyncaidh wasn't surprised Varia had turned pale. Especially at the last part—that Macurdy couldn't love any woman but his lost wife.

"Your Majesty," he said, "my wife has been ill-disposed. With your leave, I'd like to take her home. Perhaps you'll consent to see me later today."

The Emperor nodded. "By all means, Lord Cyncaidh. I'll discuss this with you promptly after lunch." He turned to Varia. "Lady Cyncaidh, I trust you'll feel better after resting."

He and the captain watched them leave, Docheri puzzled. The Cyncaidh hadn't asked one question.

She knows this Makurdi, Paedhrig told himself. *Knows him personally. If he weren't an Ozman, I'd think they'd been lovers. Well. Raien will enlighten me later. Meanwhile I'd best see the captain doesn't wonder too much.*

He looked at Docheri. "A highly intelligent woman, Lady Cyncaidh. Also fearless. And highly talented, an adept. I suspect Lord Cyncaidh has gotten her pregnant again; women can be strange in early pregnancy.

"Whatever. Let's you and I explore those military questions."

Chapter 36: Marching North

The road was a major one, graveled, wide enough for wagons to pass without risk of miring on the shoulders, and in many stretches ditched. Macurdy sat Hog in the bogus shelter of a roadside sugar maple, watching a plunder column pass. A thick soft rain fell almost too quietly to hear, had fallen for hours, and the maple dripped as copiously as the lead-gray clouds. Most of the wagons were covered, their canvas canopies streaming water like the flanks of the teams that pulled them, and the slickers of their Ozian drivers and helpers.

It was a short column; Macurdy counted nine wagons. A Kormehri plunder column had passed an hour earlier with twenty-three. This country was richer than he'd expected—much richer than Tekalos or even Indrossa—but even so, only a town could provide that much valuable plunder. More often, single wagons passed, with the take of some country manor.

He'd been out of touch with the lead cohorts, except through couriers. He'd spent two days seeing to the crossing of the rest of his army. There hadn't been a lot of fighting. After the crushing defeat of the imperial and militia cohorts at the river, more than three days and forty miles ago, the only real resistance had been outside Amotville, and that had been smashed decisively by Ozian cavalry and infantry, supported by archers of several affinities. The imperial garrison, its horses and men disorganized and decimated by heavy archery, had fought hard but briefly, and been overrun. Its militia auxiliaries had already panicked and scattered.

The Ozians too had adopted the Kormehri shout of "Ferny

Cove! Ferny Cove!" It had little significance for them, but they liked it, and bellowed it as if they came from there. And at Amotville they'd butchered imperials as freely as the Kormehri had on the night of the crossing. On the other hand, militia men who'd thrown down their weapons had been disarmed, stripped of their valuable byrnies, then freed. A policy Macurdy had propounded beginning with his early instructions to training commanders, and reiterated at every opportunity. And intended to enforce when he could.

When the plunder column had passed, Macurdy rode on, Melody with him. Other officers followed, with couriers and a platoon of Kullvordi guards. Shortly they caught and passed a cohort of Teklan infantry, mud-splashed to the knees. The soldiers recognized their commander, and his oversized horse whose name delighted them. Cheering, they waved as he rode by, some shouting "Macurdy!" and others "Hog!"

He passed through a richly mixed woods along a stream—beech and basswood, tuliptree, ash and elm, assorted maples and oaks—and out the other side. Where he saw and smelled the charred remains of a manor house, a few slicker-clad civilians poking through the rubble. Torched by a plunder company, he supposed; combat units would have had to break ranks to do it. He turned to one of the officers with him. "Bekker, ride over to those people and see if they can tell you who torched that place. Maybe they noticed the emblem on their guidon. And find out whether there were any other atrocities. Even if they don't have any information, they'll know we give a damn."

"Yessir, Marshal!" the man said, and turning his horse away, trotted toward the destruction.

Melody watched him ride off, then pulled her horse close beside her commander's. "Don't let that kind of crap get to you, Macurdy," she murmured. "It's been happening since man discovered war, and it'll keep on till he undiscovers it, if he ever does. At least you don't order it, like Quaie. If you just make it less, you can be proud."

He nodded. At Amotville, where the wounded had filled commandeered buildings, his spear maiden had been subdued by the sight and sounds. It would get worse, he knew, and told himself this wasn't just to get Varia back. Like the Great War in Europe, back on Farside, this was the war to end wars.

The problem was believing it.

* * *

The rain stopped not long after noon. The sky cleared, and by evening the ground had dried somewhat. The advance units were only a few miles ahead now; he'd catch up with them in the morning. Meanwhile reports were coming in by courier: Three Teklan companies had ridden westward, and near a place called Herrinsville had scattered a militia cohort marching east, killing "a considerable number." The Indrossan cavalry cohort had ridden eastward and chased some militia cavalry across the Travertine River. There they'd raided a hay barn and got the rain-wet bridge to burn by piling and lighting hay beneath both ends and on its planking.

It seemed unlikely to Macurdy his army's undefended corridor would become dangerous till imperial cavalry arrived from kingdoms to the east and west. Meanwhile he'd lose no sleep over it; the principal victims would likely be plunder columns. If he had to fight his way back out, *then* he'd lose sleep, though he had a plan for that, too. But the idea was to fight northward, get a treaty, and make arrangements for Varia's return, then march out peacefully.

He also received reports of a small village ravaged, with rapes and murders. And a Kullvordi company had found a plunder detachment raping the women on an estate near the road. The Kullvordi commander had arrested the sergeant and corporal of each squad and had them flogged in front of their victims, then hanged their sublieutenant and platoon sergeant from a tree by the road, their ranks conspicuous on their tunics. Each wore a crude sign reading *rapist*. The rest of the detachment he'd led off with their wagons and loot, to rejoin their own company.

Macurdy wished he'd thought to have medals struck; he could have decorated the Teklan commander. Meanwhile he'd gotten the man's name; with luck he could reward him later.

* * *

As the army continued north, the militias fought more often, though not effectively. No more imperials were seen, and someone suggested they'd abandoned the Marches, but it seemed to Macurdy that somewhere ahead they were gathering in force. Perhaps waiting for reinforcements from the north.

He rode near the front of his army now, Jeremid his operations officer. Melody was his chief of staff. One evening as they examined captured maps, an entry guard announced four Sisters. Macurdy had them shown in. Sarkia had assigned him forty of them, her most skilled magicians, she'd said. Mostly they kept inconspicuous, aided by some light spell. And by their clothing; they didn't wear the usual robes, but guardsmen's green field uniforms cut small. They had their own guard platoon, Tigers instead of ordinary guards.

The Sisters who entered his tent looked like a set of clones, and no doubt were. Their leader's name was Omara. "Marshal Macurdy," she said quietly, "are you displeased with us?"

"Displeased? No. Why?"

"You haven't called on us to help."

"Yes I have, at Big Springs. Your healing skills saved a number of lives there."

"That is not what I meant. You have not let us help you defeat enemy forces."

"We haven't needed that kind of help."

"We could have made a difference in some encounters, even though you won them easily. A mist or confusion at the right time could have saved you casualties."

Actually he'd thought of it, but didn't say so. "Sooner or later," he answered, "we'll meet an ylvin army, and if they use sorcery against us, I'll likely free you to do whatever you think will work."

She'd gazed steadily at him while they talked, no doubt observing his aura as he had hers. "Thank you, Marshal Macurdy," she said without nodding.

All four turned then without farewell, and he watched them leave. There were more than enough factors to complicate things, it seemed to him. He preferred to leave sorcery out of it, if he could.

Chapter 37: Ternass

The early morning sunlight shimmered on Macurdy's armor—the opalescent, dwarf-made byrnie and helmet Tossi Pellersson had given him, the winter past, before going off to the Silver Mountain. From his belt hung the heavy Hero's saber he'd fled Oz with, strengthened by Kittul Kendersson's dwarvish spell, and freshly honed. While Hog, he had no doubt, was the best warhorse in the army; the best to carry him at any rate.

Behind him on a slightly higher hillock, the three covens of Sisters watched, Omara their director, ready to counter any ylvin spells they detected. He'd ordered her not to initiate an exchange of magicks, and she'd said she wouldn't. Her aura showed she meant it. Sisters, he supposed, were good at obeying orders, if they accepted the authority giving them.

Off to his right, the final companies were taking their positions, and a few yards away, Jeremid sat scowling in his saddle. The Ozman didn't like Macurdy's decision to take a personal part in the fighting. "What in hell will we do if someone kills you?" he'd demanded privately. "You don't realize how important you are to this army; if we lose you, the heart'll go out of it. Going out there to cross swords with some ylf is the most stupid thing you can do!"

Macurdy hadn't argued. Basically it was true; his death here would be a disaster. But he also knew that for whatever reason, he had to take an active personal role in the fighting. Had to lay his life on the line, as he required so many others to do. He'd told this to Jeremid, and the young Ozman had simply snorted.

Now the commander stood in his stirrups, staring north

across young oats at the large Imperial force he faced. Its formation was defensive, inviting his attack, prepared to chew him up. Judging by their banners, there were four cohorts of imperial infantry alone, and massed in front of them, at least four cohorts of militia: crossbowmen protected from cavalry assault by ranks of pikemen. All of them—pikemen and crossbowmen as well as the imperial infantry—wore byrnies, and swords if it came to that kind of fight. As Macurdy intended it would.

On the enemy's right flank, imperial cavalry sat their horses, four cohorts of them as well, no doubt well trained, and all wearing byrnies. But the cavalry weren't his main concern. Not yet. Very likely the ylvin commander would hold them back until some opportunity or emergency called for them.

He wiped sweat, and wondered how good the enemy's endurance was. His own men were tough, had trained hard all winter and spring, then the infantry had hiked from wherever they lived to Kellerton or Inderstown, generally hundreds of miles. And after that, 130 miles from Parnston to Ternass. Of course, they weren't as well fed as he'd have liked; militias and civilians both had been hauling off or hiding a lot of the edibles in advance. But neither were they famished.

He studied the militia pikemen. He'd assumed something about them, an assumption based on a single observation. Their long, ungainly, simple-headed pikes were intended to stop cavalry, and that required mainly bravery and discipline. To use them against infantry, on the other hand, required considerable skill. He assumed they lacked that skill, and the confidence that would go with it.

His forces had run into pikemen just once, outside a town called Big Springs. A broad stone bridge crossed the river there, and some militia had taken a stand to defend it. Two companies of crossbowmen lined the far bank, while the bridge itself was plugged with pikemen to keep the southern cavalry from crossing. The Kormehri had charged anyway, in the teeth of deadly crossbow fire, expecting the pikemen to break and run, as militias always had. But these hadn't, and scores of Kormehri had gone down, horses and men, between the bristling pikes in front of them and the press of the oncoming ranks behind.

Even so the fanatical Kormehri had won. A single platoon of them had dismounted, swords in hand, and the pikemen had dropped their long cumbersome pikes to draw their own blades. The Kormehri platoon, greatly outnumbered, had attacked them on foot like wolves assaulting sheep, and the pikemen, previously so firm, panicked and broke, running from the bridge, even jumping armor-weighted into the river. Then Kormehri platoons still on horseback had overrun them, howling and killing; it was once when militiamen had not been allowed to surrender.

Even so, the crossbows and pikes had taken a heavy toll. When it was over, the Kormehri cavalry cohort, already short since that wild first night, reported only 264 officers and men fit for action, hardly fifty percent of those who'd crossed the river.

Actually the militias had fought harder the past two days. Not well, not even doggedly, but they'd stood and fought. He'd questioned prisoners, and they'd told him the Emperor's own army was on its way south under General Cyncaidh. They no longer felt abandoned.

The army he looked at now could hardly be the Throne Army; it wasn't big enough. Mostly these would be garrison cohorts that had withdrawn ahead of him, plus others gathered from east and west and north, with their militia auxiliaries. Macurdy squinted at the sun glinting on distant pikeheads, helmets, and mail. From beneath his own steel cap a trickle of sweat overflowed an eyebrow, but except to swipe at it with a wrist, he ignored it. *So far,* he told himself, *we've had a cakewalk, beating up on frightened militias, and on badly outnumbered imperials who didn't realize what they were up against. Here we'll learn how good we really are.*

He could, of course, have waited another day. The rest of his troops would be there by then. And the enemy seemed content to wait. But Macurdy already had the advantage of numbers, and who knew how many imperial cohorts might arrive tomorrow, or even that afternoon.

Grimly he turned to his bugler. "As planned," he said. "Mounted archers out by companies." All his cavalry were mounted archers as needed, but certain units had been assigned the role for this battle. The bugler blew, company buglers responding. Three Teklan cavalry companies trotted out in single file, briskly and without spears, not *toward* the enemy so much as across the front of its massed infantry. The imperial commander held back his cavalry, unsure what this peculiar move might mean, what might happen next. The course of the southern cavalry took them within seventy yards of the pikemen, within range of the militia crossbows. But the militiamen only gawped, their commander unsure what this meant. Again a bugle blared, and riding parallel to the enemy's front, the Teklan horsemen began to shoot, irregular flights of arrows hissing into the ranks of crouching pikemen, and the massed crossbowmen behind them. At this, the crossbowmen released their heavy bolts, and when a horseman was hit by one, whether he wore a captured byrnie or not, he fell dead or terribly wounded.

More horses than men were struck, though they went down less often. But cantering horses and their riders were poor targets at that range. The longbowmen continued to ride and shoot, circling back in a broad oval and out again. Macurdy watched, held by the sight, excited instead of horrified, his right fist jerking repeatedly with a short hooking motion. The intensity of crossbow fire had greatly lessened, due partly to casualties, but mainly to the time it took overwrought militia crossbowmen to crank their weapons, then load them if they remembered to. Now Macurdy gave another order; the bugles called the horsemen back, and sent open ranks of infantry out with longbows, jogging slowly enough not to get winded. More than a few fell to bolts before getting the order to shoot, but not till the first rank had come to about seventy yards did they stop, draw their bowstrings, and let their arrows fly. The second rank did the same, at slightly longer range, and the third and fourth, each man shooting not just once, but sending arrow after arrow—four, five, six—in the time a crossbowman took to crank his bow and shoot once.

More longbowmen jogged out then, in columns through the ranks already shooting. The columns split, spreading to form new ranks, adding to the flights of feathered death, while the crossbow fire thinned even more. Then Macurdy sent columns without bows, seven-foot stabbing spears in their fists, roaring "FERNY COVE! FERNY COVE!" at first, then simply roaring. Their ranks fragmented by casualties, the pikemen were at a disadvantage against skilled spearmen. Some dropped their unwieldy fourteen-foot pikes and big-eyed, drew their swords, further thinning the pike wall. Here and there, hearts frozen, some turned, stumbling over men behind who'd fallen to the archery, but most fought, or tried to. The roaring was pierced by screams, and after a brief minute the entire militia began to come apart, the crossbowmen dropping their bows and running, struggling and threading their way through the ylvin ranks behind them.

Only then did the ylvin commander send out two cohorts of cavalry in broad ranks, ostensibly to smash the southern infantry, though he knew the southern cavalry would intercept him. Now Macurdy, riding Hog, led out his mounted Kullvordi 2nd Cohort, strengthened by the remaining two Teklan companies. Their formation was slightly different than the ylvin—the Hero formation, densely compact, a tight shallow vee. They trotted slowly, deliberately across the battlefield, each horse almost touching the flanks of those to either side, their riders leg behind leg, shields braced, long spears gripped firmly beneath an arm. At about a hundred yards, Macurdy raised his shield overhead, a signal, and his buglers blew the charge. The whole formation broke into a canter at almost the same instant as the imperial cavalry.

They crashed together, and it was the Kullvordi and Teklar, with their more compact formation, who drove through, horses stumbling over fallen horses, trampling fallen men. Then spears were dropped, sabers drawn, and the melee truly begun.

Back across the oat field, Jeremid watched, prepared to react to any further ylvin cavalry move. He had three cohorts of cavalry available, plus the three companies of mounted Teklar with bows. Meanwhile more ranks of southern foot troops jogged across the trampled oats to engage the ylvin infantry.

Macurdy's heavy Ozian saber slashed and thrust as if it had some dervish spirit of its own. His shield was heavier than the others, its steel bands broader and thicker, and it seemed always where it needed to be.

The ylver by and large were better swordsmen, but with ranks broken by the charge, they fought mostly as individuals. Macurdy dominated wherever he was, and with two picked sergeants, went where most needed. After a few minutes, the ylver began an organized disengagement, back to the small hill from which they'd ridden. Macurdy looked around for his bugler and couldn't find him, so he shouted his order, other voices repeating it: "To base! To base!" Company buglers heard and blew it, and as they started back toward the rise they'd ridden from, squads and platoons began reforming on their guidons, while a bugler worked his way toward his marshal, to serve him.

Almost at once they saw another cavalry battle, a cohort from each army. Macurdy bellowed "*Engage*," and spurred Hog into a brisk trot. The nearest bugler heard and blew. Some of the cohort took a moment to realize the situation and respond, but within seconds they all were headed at a trot for the other fight, still reforming units. Some of the ylver heard them coming. An ylvin trumpet called, and ylvin troopers, those who could, disengaged and retreated; others fought and died. At the same time, Jeremid and the ylvin commander both threw their remaining cohorts toward each other in an orderly charge.

For an indeterminate time Macurdy fought, while men and ylver fell. Twice he saved his new bugler without being consciously aware of it. A saber struck his dwarf-made byrnie hard, and once a blow on his helmet blurred his vision, making his mouth taste of blood.

Finally the last ylvin cohort disengaged, and mostly his men let them go, for they too were exhausted. Hoarsely he called an order to his bugler. The man blew, and the cohort, all the cohorts, trotted their horses back to the hillock, again reforming as they rode, for it was drilled into them. They were too spent to feel exhilarated.

Macurdy was one of the last to leave, looking toward the site of the infantry battle as he rode. It too was over, had been for a while. His infantry had substantially outnumbered the ylvin and militia infantry to begin with, and when the militia broke, it left the ylver at a severe disadvantage, despite their byrnies and training. After heavy slugging, they'd withdrawn, leaving their dead and wounded to the badly reduced southerners.

Macurdy found Jeremid back before him; the Ozman had ridden out with the last cohort committed, and was grinning ear to ear, his byrnie splashed with blood not his own. "You look like a butcher, Macurdy!" he called in greeting.

Macurdy looked down and found himself bloodier than Jeremid. "Get me something white!" he shouted.

"White?"

"I want to parley with the imperial commander."

"Something white!" someone called. "Get the marshal something white!" The call spread through the cohorts, but no one came forth with anything white. Macurdy trotted his horse back onto the battlefield, where leaning far down, he snatched a fallen spear on the trot, and put his helmet on its point. Holding it high, he trotted Hog toward the little hill.

The ylver commander watched him come, making no move to meet him. At fifty yards, Macurdy stopped. "A truce!" he shouted. "A truce!"

The ylvin general rode out then, his youthful face grim. At twenty yards he too stopped.

"To what end?"

"To do what we can for the wounded!"

For a long moment the ylf stared. "Have you surgeons?"

"And Sisters; healers. I suppose you have your own."

The ylf nodded. "A truce then. Till when?"

Macurdy's face worked. >*From now on,* he thought. *Forever.* "Until sunrise tomorrow."

"A truce till sunrise. Agreed." The ylvin general trotted back to his staff, and Macurdy turned toward his. Partway there, he could hear ylvin trumpets, presumably signaling the truce, for the general's aura had shown no sign of treachery. The southern army had no bugle call for a truce, so when he reached his own men, Macurdy sent couriers to inform the cohorts.

And one to bring the Sisters. They trotted their horses to

him, their Tiger platoon riding straight-backed and expression-less behind them. Macurdy sent them out to where hundreds on hundreds—thousands!—of dead and wounded strewed the ground, then looked around and spoke to Jeremid. "Where's Melody?"

The Ozman's face fell. "Shit!" he said, scanning around. "I told her to stay here! That she was in charge till I got back!"

"I'll find her," Macurdy said. "Get litter bearers organized; what we've got aren't nearly enough. And commandeer build-ings in Ternass for the wounded."

Then he ordered a courier to follow him, and rode out to the last place they'd fought. If Melody was alive, that was probably where she'd be. He went to her like a needle to a magnet, found her sprawled across a dead horse, still and bloody as a corpse. From thirty feet distant, he wanted to die, for he could see no aura. When he reached her, he swung from his saddle. There was an aura after all, thin and dull. Her face was ash pale, her splash of freckles a contrast and alarm. Simply removing her badly dented helmet strengthened her aura. He raised her a bit, and with the courier's help, pulled off her byrnie. Seemingly the blood was not her own, for there was no visible wound.

"Bring a litter," he ordered, then watched the courier mount and canter off.

* * *

When she'd been taken away, Macurdy looked around. His impulse was to take one end of a makeshift litter and help carry, but there were many who could do that. His job was to be in charge. Not that he was much good at it just then; Jeremid gave the orders. Much of the time, Macurdy sat silent and motionless in the saddle, watching litter bearers; carters stripping byrnies from the dead and gathering weapons; and after a bit, crews of surrendered militiamen and his own troops hauling and stacking wood and straw for funeral pyres.

Near noon, he rode to the house where Melody had been taken, one of numerous filled with wounded. As chief of staff, and assumed to be their commander's lover, she'd been put in a small room by herself. He found her there in bed, conscious but groggy, head aching. She didn't remember the battle at all; didn't even remember getting up that morning. Macurdy kissed her forehead and told her she'd be all right. Meanwhile she was to stay in bed; that was an order.

Sisters moved through the houses, touching, murmuring chants. He assigned a surly-faced Ozian corporal to stay outside Melody's door, with orders no Sister was to have access to her. He couldn't have said why.

Meanwhile the enemy had ridden away northward, their wounded in a train of crowded wagons. The base they left behind, Fort Ternass, wasn't much of a fort. Far too small for so large an army, its walls might keep out vagrants, but they'd be little obstacle to a military assault. As soon as it had been vacated, Jeremid had a Miskmehri infantry cohort occupy it.

The ylvin departure drew Macurdy out of his numbness, and he sent an order for his senior staff to meet with him. While he waited, he unrolled a captured imperial military map. Just a few miles north, it showed a broad stretch of country liberally marked with wetland symbols. The road continued north through it. Six miles to both east and west, other roads crossed it; eight or ten miles beyond them, the wetland symbols disappeared.

Macurdy stood silent a few moments, thinking. The army they'd fought that day would no doubt join forces with the Throne Army riding south. An army by itself too large for him to deal with, reportedly a full legion of cavalry and another of mounted infantry. Under its General Cyncaidh, his wife's captor, who when he was at home, no doubt took her to his bed at night.

He shook the thought off, and wished Blue Wing was with him. But the great raven had left near winter's end, for his tribe's rookery in the Great Eastern Mountains. It wouldn't do to take sides in such a war. And he'd never had a mate, he told Macurdy, never raised nestlings. It seemed time.

When Macurdy's staff had gathered, they quieted on their own. "Somewhere north of the marshes," Macurdy said, "there's an ylvin army riding south, and the people we fought this morning will be joining it. We don't know when they'll get here." He looked at his operations officer. "Jeremid, what are the swamps like ahead?"

"The only patrol that's back so far followed the road to the other side and came straight back. It's five or six miles across, mostly cattail marsh, with creeks and open pools. Impossible to cross, even on foot. But the road? You'd have to see it to believe it. It's not only ditched; it's got a raised bed of rock, packed with dirt and topped with gravel."

Macurdy examined the map again. If he continued north with his army, they'd face a much larger ylvin army, with the marshes between themselves and escape, and only the road to funnel out on. And with the likelihood of more ylvin cohorts hitting them from east and west later. While if they stayed where they were, holding the marsh roads, the ylver could bypass the marshes. It might take them a couple of days.

He could, of course, turn around in the morning and head south, leaving rear guards to block the roads, giving the rest of the army a start. It was doubtful the imperials would catch them north of the Big River. Not in force.

For a moment that seemed to be the answer: Get south of the Big River with his army. Then he remembered his purpose—why he was there. South of the river wouldn't get Varia back, nor put him in position to bargain with the emperor. Anxiety flooded. *And say we arrive at the river a day ahead of the ylver: What then? There's no fleet of boats waiting. We'll be trapped! They'll capture thousands. First they'll murder the prisoners and wounded, then they'll cross the river and rape the Rude Lands.* Anxiety became despair. *You've deluded yourself,* he thought, *and Wollerda, and everyone else who trusted you. There was never any prospect of a treaty. Your blind determination to get Varia back has already killed thousands, and thousands more will die before it's over.*

Then abruptly, snarling, another part of him rose up. *Bullshit, Macurdy. Make things happen!*

"Jeremid! I want a platoon from the 2nd, ready at sunup in presentable uniforms. And couriers, and an Alliance flag, and a flag of truce. They'll ride north with me. Pick up the pikes the militia dropped today, and arm some companies with them. Make sure they know how to use them. Assign two companies of infantry and one of cavalry to plug each of the roads."

Jeremid nodded, steady as a rock. "Right."

"Round up wagons. Start the wounded south as soon as they can travel. Commandeer all the civilian wagons you need. And the plunder wagons; we've sent enough plunder down the road. And send couriers to Kithro—separately, in case they run into trouble. Get them started right away and tell them to push it. Tell Kithro we'll be wanting boats again soon.

"I'll ride north to find the enemy commander. The only real ylvin army we've met so far, we've thrashed. It's time to parley, while we're winners."

He scanned the rest of his staff. "Any comments or questions?"

All except Jeremid looked very sober, but only one spoke: "You'll be a long way from help, Marshal. Suppose they don't respect your flag of truce?"

"I heard several days ago their commander is General Cyncaidh. And I know a little about him. He's said to be an honorable man; certainly he's not another Quaie."

He waited, and when no one else spoke, dismissed them.

* * *

After the staff meeting, Macurdy visited the wounded again. Melody was sleeping, and he didn't disturb her. Her aura was much stronger.

The army had brought "surgeons" with it—sawbones actually—one per cohort, and shamans and other healers of greater or lesser talent and skill. But judging by auras, the men in buildings assigned to ministration by Sisters were in notably better condition. Macurdy went to the officer in charge, an Indrossan, and took him aside.

"Major, are you aware I'm a magician?"

"It is general knowledge, Marshal Macurdy." The Indrossan was grave-faced.

"Have you noticed any difference between the wounded treated by the Sisters, and the rest of them?"

"No sir."

He may have some skills, Macurdy told himself, *but not much talent.* "They're doing a lot better," he said. "Their auras show it."

The major said nothing, but his aura showed disbelief, whether of auras or the Sisters' better results wasn't apparent.

"I'm going to have them minister to the rest of the men."

The man looked stricken. "I— Marshal, Sisters can't be trusted!"

Macurdy laid a large hand on the major's shoulder. "You've had a hard day. When did you eat last?"

"I had an orderly bring me bread and meat at noon."

"Get something to eat, and walk around outdoors. Don't come back till tomorrow. That's an order."

The major looked near tears.

"You know about orders. Eat something and walk around camp. Look at something besides broken bodies. Have a drink, then get some sleep." He put a hand on the major's back, herding him along, and they left the building together.

* * *

It was Omara herself whom he took to see Melody. She'd tried before to see her, she told him, but a soldier had kept her out. "At your orders, Marshal. You distrust me. Why?"

"It's nothing personal," he said, and opened the door. Omara went to the bed and looked at the sleeping spear maiden for a long moment, *examining her aura,* he thought. "She doesn't need me," she told him. "By this time tomorrow she'll be largely recovered, though she should rest at least another day."

She looked at him coolly. "You are an enigma, Macurdy, a talented enigma."

"Enigma. That's a word I haven't met. But distrust now...I suppose Sarkia told you my experience with the Sisterhood. I like and respect you, Omara, but you'll excuse me if I have the colonel's guard refuse you entrance to this room except when I'm with you."

"Marshal, I have enough to do without troubling someone who doesn't need me."

They left Melody then, Omara going on to visit other patients. Macurdy paused outside Melody's door, talking with the man on guard, then left for supper. *Sarkia never believed you'd get Varia back,* he told himself, *regardless of what she said. And you're the most powerful leader in the Rude Lands; she'd love to marry you to a Sister. If she thought Melody might stand in the way, or maybe even if Omara thought so…*

* * *

He'd taken off his hillsman boots and was washing his socks when his Kullvordi orderly looked in. "Marshal, sir! Major Tarlok wants to see you! Says it's urgent!"

Tarlok was peering in over the man's shoulder. "What is it, Tarlok?"

"A bunch of Kormehri grabbed some local women. They were carrying them to their camp. I thought you should know."

Macurdy swore and pulled on his boots, not taking time for socks.

"You want me to get a company or two, in case there's trouble?"

"No. If I showed up with a bunch of men, there'd be trouble for sure. But you can come with me if you'd like."

He tied the laces around his ankles, belted on his saber, and left the tent at a trot, Tarlok with him. Both were unaccustomed to running, and Macurdy slowed before they got there so he wouldn't arrive gasping for breath. It was twilight, nearly dark, but he knew where in the Kormehri camp to go by the cheering, and found a crowd gathered on a company muster ground. He couldn't see what was going on—the circle was several men deep, most without their breeches—but he pushed through, Tarlok with him. A fire had been built in the middle for light. More than a dozen women and girls had been stripped, forced to hands and knees, and their wrists tied to stakes. All of them were occupied. He didn't hesitate, but strode to the nearest man, grabbed him by the hair and jerked him backward. The crowd went still, all but the man he'd interrupted, who scrambled to his feet swearing vividly. To find a saber tip at his solar plexus.

"YOU SON OF A BITCH!" Macurdy bellowed, and abruptly, with a backhanded wrist movement, slapped the side of the man's face with the flat of his blade. The man stepped back, hand to cheek, aware now whom he faced, and that he'd been only a turn of the wrist from death. The other rapists had dismounted and backed away, staring with varying degrees of anger and fear. Macurdy and Tarlok strode around the circle cutting ropes, freeing the women.

Macurdy straightened and looked around. "Where are their clothes?"

The company commander stepped into the circle then. He wore no breeches, but his sword was in his hand. "This is my company!" he shouted. "What goes on here is none of your business!"

The place was doubly still now. Macurdy walked slowly toward him. "Do you challenge me, you dog turd?"

The Kormehri took half a step backward before he realized what he was doing, then with an oath, rushed at Macurdy. Their blades met violently—and the Kormehri's snapped. Macurdy thrust him through and let him fall.

The crowd remained quiet as Quakers. "What company is this?" Macurdy shouted.

"Barlin's Company," someone answered.

"Barlin's Company fall in!" he ordered.

Most of the men moved as if to form ranks. But not all, and a sergeant drew his sword. "You might kill one of us, you Ozian pig," he shouted, "but you can't—"

He stopped in midsentence. Macurdy said nothing, simply stalked toward him, drilling him with his eyes—and just off the tip of his saber was a ball of white fire the size of an egg. The man stared at it transfixed, and screamed when Macurdy thrust him through.

"Barlin's Company, *fall in!*" Macurdy repeated, and this time there was a general scramble to obey. "Major Tarlok," he called, "help the women find their clothes."

Most of the men stood in ranks now, but a few, perhaps a dozen, were slipping away into the darkness. "*Stop where you are!*"

Most stopped, though several fled.

"Where were you men going?"

"Back to our company, Marshal," one called apologetically. "We're not Barlin's, sir. We just came to see what was going on."

Yeah, and have a turn at it. "All right," he called. "Just remember what you saw and heard." He turned his attention back to Barlin's Company, a company short by at least a third, no doubt from the morning's battle…and felt his anger die. "Do you know why I killed your captain?" he asked. "And your sergeant?" His voice, though loud, was almost conversational. Suddenly it boomed. "BECAUSE THEY DEFIED ME. DEFIED MY ORDERS! Now let me remind you: I gave orders that there is to be no raping. Your captain and your sergeant defied those orders. Now they're dead! Sent to Hell!"

His eyes found Tarlok again. And the women, now with their torn and trampled clothing clutched to them. "Major, take these women to the Sisters. Tell Omara what happened; tell her to do something for them. And get them some clothes; Barlin's Company will pay for them."

He turned to the men in ranks. "Company, 'ten*tion!* Right *face!* Forward *march!*" Calling cadence, he marched them out of the firelight, through the night to the battlefield, most of them barefoot and without pants. On the bloody killing ground, he double-timed them back and forth, controlling them from a central position, for he'd become so much a horseman, he'd done no serious walking for months, let alone running. While they were infantry, their legs tough, their lungs like bellows. After about twenty minutes he marched them back, but before he dismissed them, he asked who'd been second in command.

A tall, rawboned man spoke up. "I was, sir."

"What's your name?"

"Arliss, lieutenant, Second Kormehri Infantry, sir."

"Lieutenant, you are now a captain, and company commander. Congratulations on a first class company. But remember…" Abruptly his voice raised to a roar. "NO RAPING! AND NO MURDERING CIVILIANS! I don't want to send any more of you to Hell." He paused. "I'm turning them over to you now,

Captain. Take up a collection for the women, tonight. Every man *will* give something. Something valuable, whatever he has."

With that, he turned and strode out of the firelight.

* * *

>From the Kormehri bivouac area, he went back to look in on Melody again. She'd been awake, or on the verge of it, because when he stepped in, her head turned, eyes open. "Hello, Macurdy," she murmured. "Where have you been?"

"Here, a few times. The last two you were asleep, and the first time you didn't know where you were or what had happened."

"Want to feel my lump?"

"Sure." He knelt, and his fingers touched her head. "Pretty good one."

She chuckled weakly.

"How's your headache?"

"Not bad. But when I got up to use my bucket, a little while ago, I was pretty dizzy."

"I had a Sister look at you. She said you'll be a lot better tomorrow, but you need to stay in bed a day or two more."

She looked thoughtful for a moment. "You know what's really good for someone in my condition?"

"I'm afraid to ask."

"Remember what I did for you after you got beaten up so badly?"

He nodded.

"If you'd do something like that for me..."

He bent and kissed her cheek. "Not now."

"When, then?"

"Sometime. Soon. If we get through this war alive."

"Do you mean it?"

Again he nodded.

"Will you marry me?" she asked.

He felt his head going up and down as if it had a will of its own.

"Kiss me," she said. "On the mouth. To make it real."

He did, softly, sweetly.

"I feel stronger already, Macurdy."

He stood up. "Go back to sleep, spear maiden."

Obediently she closed her eyes, and turning, he padded quietly from the room. Feeling like a wooden man, wondering how he could possibly have said what he had.

Chapter 38: Lord Quaie

Cyncaidh rode erect but relaxed at the head of his staff, on a smooth-gaited stallion that would not have tolerated an ordinary rider. In front of him, the Emperor's elite 1st Cavalry Cohort filled the road almost to the top of the next rise. Two complete legions followed, twenty cohorts of cavalry and mounted infantry with their supply trains, a great cumbersome dragon extending for miles, its serpentine body integrated by well-drilled protocol and couriers on horseback.

He sniffed, and smiled ruefully. A morning like this should smell of wildflowers and meadow grass, but already the odors of horse urine and trampled manure dominated. At the rear of the column, the road would be nearly mired with it. If the breeze would just swing round to the east or west, instead of holding from the south...From the south. He wondered how yesterday's battlefield smelled, after a day of sunshine, warmth, and flies. Mearigher's casualty report, delivered by courier the day before had been bad enough, but to actually see the remnant of Mearigher's army with its hospital train this morning had been powerfully sobering.

It truly was astonishing that an effective southern army had been assembled from so many different nations. And by a farmer from Farside, with no previous experience of war or leadership in this lifetime.

A marsh hawk caught Cyncaidh's eye, soaring low over the meadow beside the road, single-minded, oblivious to the army. It slowed, and with blurred wing strokes hovered a moment, then dropped into the tangle of grass and forbs, to fly up with a rodent in its claws. Nature too had its violence, he reminded himself, but seemingly little more than needed to eat and raise young. Only men and ylver fertilized their fields with blood from time to time. Their great challenge, laid on them by God, was to change, he had no doubt. Change, and lose their bloodiness; change by dint of growing wisdom. Meanwhile one did the best one could, dealing with the world as it was.

Ahead, a courier rode toward him against the direction of march, cantering his horse briskly along the road's edge. The rider, a sublieutenant, kept his pace almost until he'd reached Cyncaidh, then stopped, saluted, and turned his horse to ride alongside the general. "Sir!" he said. "The point's met a small force of southerners ahead, under a flag of truce. With a man who says he's Marshal Makurdi."

"Aha!" The voice was Quaie's, calling from behind him. "You'll have him in your hands, Cyncaidh! Don't waste the opportunity!"

The admonition irritated the commander, and half turning in the saddle, he glanced back. Disregarding his aura, the seventy-year-old Rapist of Ferny Cove looked like a handsome youth: tall, slender, impeccably tailored, and utterly hairless, with refined features. But his eyes invariably showed contempt, while the mouth was inclined to mock or smirk. Quaie had been against Paedhrig's orders to negotiate if possible, and had been taking it out on his chief counselor. *May you be reborn as a maggot in your own carcass!* Cyncaidh thought.

As commander, Cyncaidh could always stomp on him, but politically it would be unwise. Better to let the war erode his influence, already shrunken by Ferny Cove.

He glanced at Varia on his right. Her aura had receded and paled at the report, but only a little. "What's the ground like ahead?" he asked the sublieutenant.

"Much the same as here, General."

He sent the man cantering back up to the route leader with orders to stop for an indefinite break, then sent similar orders to the other cohorts. And thought his apologies to the farmers whose crops would be trampled by his camping army. "I'll have the headquarters tent set up," he told his staff. "We'll see what this Macurdy has to say. If he's come to negotiate, we may spend a day or two here."

He ignored Quaie's remark: "Why set up the tent? A sharpened stake in the hot sun would be more appropriate."

* * *

The tent was up before the southern commander arrived. If necessary he'd have had Macurdy delayed to get it done. It would seriously jeopardize negotiations if the man saw Varia. As it was, she could listen from behind the linen wall while watching through the spy hole, and he'd consult with her during breaks.

The large staff room had panels rolled up on two sides for ventilation, and Cyncaidh and his general staff lounged around a trestle table with a top of intricate parquetry. He wondered what Curtis Macurdy would think of it, or if he'd notice. Outside, a horse cantered up and stopped; a moment later the sublieutenant stepped inside and saluted.

"He's almost here, General."

Cyncaidh got to his feet, his staff following suit, Quaie sneering something about the disgrace of fawning on a criminal like that. *You're our expert on disgrace,* Cyncaidh thought, and led them outside. From there he could see the southern commander, a big man with big shoulders, on a big horse. With no spear maiden by him, nor any aide at all. His platoon was being guided to the pastured grove set aside to shelter them from the sun, leaving him alone with his ylvin escort. No doubt his men were less than happy with that, Cyncaidh told himself.

Macurdy dismounted, his movements easy, casually athletic. He wore neither byrnie nor helmet. His hair was short-bobbed, the color of wet sand, and as he neared, his eyes showed hazel. His hands, Cyncaidh thought, might be the largest he'd seen. His aura showed more than power and honesty; there was also what Cyncaidh read as purpose and logic, care and concern.

And inborn dominance. The ylver didn't have a specific classification of personality types, as expressed in auras, but he recognized the aura of a man born to command, and the strong aural fullness of one who did. He stopped in front of Cyncaidh. "My name is Macurdy," he said. "I'm the commander of the southern alliance."

Cyncaidh nodded gravely. "I am General Cyncaidh." He gestured at the tent. "Step inside and we'll talk."

They went in together, Cyncaidh's staff following. An orderly held a chair for Macurdy, as instructed. It would give Varia a view of him in profile, while avoiding any chance he'd see an eye behind the spy hole. When everyone was seated, Cyncaidh asked, "Why have you come to us, Commander?"

"There were two things," Macurdy said, "that I was supposed to do on this campaign. One was to punish the empire for laying waste to Kormehr, and for the Rape at Ferny Cove. The other was to get a treaty of peace to last forever, with a pledge of trade without tariffs, and an exchange of ambassadors. I've been told you're the emperor's chief counselor; I came to talk terms."

Quaie snorted derisively, drawing annoyed glances from the rest of the staff and a sharp look from Cyncaidh.

"You understand," Cyncaidh said, "that my authority is limited. Any terms we might work out will be tentative, pending the emperor's signature. Who on your side needs to sign?"

"Just me. My authority's good."

In the name of all those kings and chiefs?! Even with the Dynast behind the man, Cyncaidh was surprised. And momentarily uncomfortable with it. It greatly expedited matters, but it felt—almost indecent for things to be so simple. "Are you hungry, Commander?" he asked. "Perhaps you'd like lunch first."

"I ate in the saddle."

"Then I suggest we begin an exploratory discussion now."

"Good. I'm ready."

One might almost be hopeful, Cyncaidh told himself. *No arrogance, no posturing, no petty jockeying.* He gestured at the men around the table. "While the authority here is mine, Commander, these lords may have questions or suggestions, or information to contribute, and they will witness any tentative agreement we may come to. On my left are Lord General A'raiel, Lord General Quaie..."

At Quaie's name, Macurdy got so abruptly to his feet, he knocked over his folding chair, freezing the others where they sat. "You expect me to sit down with the Butcher of Kormehr? The Rapist of Ferny Cove?" He hawked, and spat on the floor. Quaie sent his own chair toppling backward then, hand on his saber hilt. Macurdy, in response, reached for his.

For just an instant Cyncaidh was dismayed, then realized neither man's aura showed rage. Macurdy's showed what might be satisfaction, Quaie's restrained glee. Cyncaidh understood Quaie's motivation: the man was famous as a fencer, a master of the saber.

"My lords!" he said sharply, "control yourselves!"

Each man stopped short of drawing his weapon.

"This peasant has insulted me in words and act," Quaie answered coldly, then turned his glare to Macurdy. "I challenge you to duel."

Cyncaidh was prepared to veto this; he had the authority, and the political repercussions of frustrating Quaie's bloody intention were far more acceptable than those of Macurdy's death. And surely Quaie would win. "My lords—" he began firmly, but Macurdy overrode the words.

"Among civilized people," Macurdy said, "if one challenges, the other chooses the weapon. Are you civilized, Quaie?"

Cyncaidh held back then. Macurdy had something in mind. Best to wait, see what this meant, and step in later if need be.

Quaie was taken aback for only a moment, for he was an expert at spear fencing too, and no other alternative occurred to him. He smiled mockingly. "By all means, human. I've been training and dueling for more years than you've lived. Choose as you wish."

Macurdy held up his large hands, thick palmed, the fingers hooked. "Hands," he said calmly. "We'll fight with bare hands."

Cyncaidh expected Quaie to refuse. Wrestling was popular among ylver in preadolescence, but not later, while fist fighting was considered uncouth, suited only to slaves. And Macurdy was clearly far stronger than Quaie. So the ylf lord's answer bewildered Cyncaidh. "Perfect! Perfect!" Qauie said. "Hands it will be!"

"My lords," Cyncaidh said firmly, "I cannot allow this."

It was Macurdy, not Quaie, who foiled him. "Chief Counselor," he said, "if you disallow this, I'll ride back to my army today."

Quaie smirked. "Indeed, Lord General, let the boy take his punishment. He will learn from it." Then he turned and walked out the door, Macurdy close behind. And for almost the first time since adolescence, Cyncaidh had no notion of what to do in a situation. He simply followed them into the sunshine, his staff dumbfounded at his heels.

"And how," said Quaie, "do we decide the victor? Shall we fight till one of us cannot continue? Or surrenders? I do owe you the option of quitting, I suppose."

"We fight till one is dead," Macurdy answered.

"Ah. To the death then." Quaie removed his tunic and undershirt, Macurdy following suit. Then they faced off, Quaie tall, slender and sinewy, Macurdy nearly as tall and strongly muscled. Cyncaidh had no idea what Quaie had in mind. His fists weren't even clenched; his hands were poised half open.

"Tell me when you're ready," Quaie said.

"I'm ready."

Quaie stepped forward, at the same time ducking, and his left hand darted toward Macurdy. Macurdy's right fist drove in a compact, hooking arc, striking Quaie hard on the side of the face, smashing him backward. For a long moment the ylf sat stunned and blinking on the ground, blood trickling from a gash on one cheekbone. Even before he got to his feet, the cheek had begun to darken and swell, as if the bone was broken. And the smirk was gone; Cyncaidh saw fear and rage in Quaie's aura now.

"Always look up, Quaie," Macurdy said mildly.

When Quaie got up, Macurdy moved in again. A hammer fist shot out, striking Quaie on the nose, and once more the ylf went down hard, blood flowing freely.

"That's called a left jab. The one before was a right hook."

Quaie stayed down seconds longer this time, gathering his

wits and resolution, then rolled to hands and knees as if to get up. But instead, as he began to rise, he lunged at Macurdy's legs. Macurdy started to step backward, but Quaie grabbed his left knee with both hands—and Macurdy roared with pain, flinging backward and landing on his buttocks.

Now it was Quaie who stood. Shock fingers! Clearly his talent went well beyond the ylvin norm, regardless of his public attitude. And to interfere now, after the humiliation and injuries he'd suffered, would bring severe censure, Cyncaidh realized, even from the many who disliked Quaie. The Emperor would have no choice but to dismiss him, not only as chief counselor, but from the Council and military command.

Blood flowing from his nose, Quaie began to circle Macurdy. "You see," he said, "the hands are good for more than striking blows." Macurdy swiveled on his tailbone as if to kick out in defense. Quaie feinted a grab, drew a kick by Macurdy's right foot, and snatched it. Again Macurdy roared with pain, rocking backward.

Quaie let him go and began circling again. Macurdy, pale and twitching, had trouble pivoting now. Quaie could easily have gone for his temples, where the shock would have killed, but he preferred to gloat first. "I've heard that shock fingers applied to the genitals shrivel them forever. When I've paralyzed you, Commander, I'll try it."

Cyncaidh took a single step toward Quaie; shock fingers couldn't harm him, prepared as he was, and he couldn't let this continue, regardless of the consequences to himself. But he moved too late. Macurdy, still dazed, had raised a hand toward Quaie—and from it a fist-sized ball of glowing plasma appeared! For just an instant it floated there, then shot out to strike the ylf in the midriff. Quaie shrieked and flung backward, his abdomen a gaping, steaming, messy hole, to lie bulge-eyed, conspicuously, bonelessly dead. The onlookers stood stunned, slack-jawed.

More than Cyncaidh and his staff had witnessed the fight and its uncanny finish. Various soldiers, though keeping their distance, had paused in their activities to watch and listen more or less covertly. Now they stood frozen, mouths open. Cyncaidh, suddenly aware of them, shouted, "Soldiers! If you have things to do, get about them! If you don't, I'll see you're given some!"

They scurried like rabbits.

"Sergeant Glinnoch! Get a litter! Have General Quaie taken to the surgeon!" *Who can declare him officially dead.* "Captain Flion! Pass the order that we camp here tonight!"

Then he himself stepped to Macurdy, who sat staring at the ruined corpse. "Are you able to stand, Commander?"

Macurdy pulled his attention from what had been Quaie. "Not without help," he husked. "My legs are weak as noodles."

* * *

Cyncaidh had a second litter brought, and Macurdy, quaking now with aftershock, was lain on a pallet beneath a shady tree, and an ylvin healer sent for. Then Cyncaidh seated his staff as a committee of evidence, to draft a statement they all agreed on, describing Quaie's death and how it happened. They'd all witnessed it, and there were no disagreements on what had been said or done. They also agreed on the legality of the duel, that it was Quaie who'd issued the challenge and been first to use magic, and that when Macurdy had seemed helpless, Quaie had said he was going to mutilate him.

On the other hand, Quaie had issued his challenge only after Macurdy had called him the Rapist of Ferny Cove, and had emphasized his scorn by spitting on the ground.

Given the unanimity of the general staff, Quaie's aide, who'd also been sworn in as part of the committee, could hardly avoid signing a statement of witnessed evidence. But he added a complaint that Macurdy's tone, in speaking to Quaie, had been insulting in the extreme. Cyncaidh then added a rejoinder, pointing out that considering the extremity of Quaie's actions in Kormehr, and the intensity of southern feelings, Macurdy's having spat only on the ground could be regarded as an exercise in restraint.

Actually, Quaie had been called the Rapist of Ferny Cove by more than a few of his peers, some of them publicly. There'd be a fuss, and some long-lasting bitterness, but by persons who already hated both himself and the Emperor. Certainly the situation would be far less serious than he'd anticipated during the fight.

When the committee of evidence had completed and signed their statement, the scribe took it to another room to write copies, before the original was sent off to Duinarog. Then Macurdy was brought in, on his feet now, supported by two ylvin soldiers. After a lunch eaten at the conference table, they began discussing the basic features of a peace agreement. Cyncaidh had felt optimistic, but hadn't expected it to go as smoothly as it did. He and Macurdy had similar ideas of what was desirable and just.

They didn't break for supper, but ate again at the conference table, still discussing. Finally Cyncaidh suggested they stop for the evening. His scribe could organize their discussion as a draft agreement for review in the morning. It seemed to him probable that never in the history of the empire had a major agreement, nor many minor agreements, been worked out to mutual satisfaction so quickly.

"Fine," Macurdy said. "But before we sleep, there's something you and I need to talk about, unrelated to the treaty. A personal ambition I have."

Cyncaidh frowned. "Very well, Commander. I'll have our horses saddled and we can take a ride." He turned to his general staff. "Gentlemen, you are dismissed. We'll meet again after breakfast."

The two commanders watched the others file out. Then Cyncaidh turned to the couriers and door guards. "You too," he said. "All but you, Alhnar. I want you to have our horses saddled and brought to us." When they were gone, he spoke to Macurdy in an undertone little louder than a whisper. "We have a few minutes to wait. What is this all about, Commander? Not the details, but the major matter."

Macurdy too spoke in a murmur. "I'm a married man, general. My wife, who was a Sister, was stolen from me, and after a time passed into ylvin hands. Your hands personally: I'm told she's your slave now, or has been, and I want her back. But if your staff knew, someone might say you'd given in on points of the agreement because of it. And I don't want anything to threaten that. Too many have died for it."

Cyncaidh stared for a long moment while Macurdy waited. Finally, in a normal voice, he said, "Excuse me, Commander. Let me call my wife; she may be able to advise us. Varia, would you come out please? We'd like you to take a ride with us."

Varia! It was Macurdy's turn to stare, open-mouthed. The curtain moved at the rear of the room, and Varia stepped out. He felt as if his windpipe had locked; his throat hurt from the constriction. She was more beautiful than he'd recalled. "I'll need to change into riding clothes first," she said, not meeting Macurdy's eyes. Then she disappeared again.

* * *

She didn't reappear till Cyncaidh called that her horse was there. Then the three of them left the tent, mounted, and rode to the road, all without speaking. A slender moon hung low in the west, while in the east, the first stars climbed the darkening sky. It was Macurdy who spoke first, in American, his voice thick. "Are you really married to him?"

She answered in Yuultal. "Yes. In this world."

A confusion of thoughts flooded his mind, but no words came to him. It was Cyncaidh who spoke. "Let me tell you what might be difficult for her to say." As they rode, Cyncaidh told briefly how he'd found her. Of her assault on him when he refused to take her to Ferny Cove, or let her go alone. Chuckling as he finished. "If ylver scarred as men do, I'd still bear the marks on my face."

He went on from there: how she'd learned of his love, and nearly drowned trying to escape. And how he and Mariil had teamed up to overcome her resistance. "You might well hold a deep grudge against me, Curtis Macurdy. For if I'd determined to, it's quite possible I could have gotten her safely to the Oz Gate. But if she'd gotten back to Farside, she wouldn't have found you, because you were here. It's only because we did what we did that you've met again."

Macurdy didn't answer, simply turned his gaze to her and found her watching him. "I can get our children back for us," he said. "It's part of my agreement with Sarkia."

By moonlight, her eyes gleamed with tears. "Oh Curtis, so much has happened. So much has changed! I've changed, a lot, and you even more. And Raien and I have a baby, a beautiful child. And what he told you isn't all there is to tell. I knew early on I loved him, and couldn't face it. Couldn't face what it meant."

"Do you want to be with him then, instead of me?"

She turned her eyes ahead, not answering for a bit, and when she spoke, she still didn't answer. Instead she told in a low monotone of her trip to the gate and the Cloister, not omitting Xader's harassments and death. Of her year there, the Tiger barracks, the rapes, her escape and recapture.

"I know some of it, a little," Macurdy said. And told her what he'd learned from Jeremid about Xader's death. Told her briefly of Liiset's lies, and the tomttu's. And what the skull had shown him, the skull that had to be Tomm's.

She was staring at him now. "I could see you had talent," she said, "but even after I'd explored it, I didn't imagine how strong it was. What you did to Quaie today—I've never heard of anything like that.

"We were innocents when we married. Our dream of farming in Illinois couldn't work now, Curtis.

"And Raien has a dream too, one I've come to share. The same dream you worked on today at the conference table: of a peace held in place by treaty and trade and embassies. But the agreement's only a first step; none of us will see the dream complete in this lifetime. Imperial government needs to become more rational, its politics more ethical, our people wiser. That's another part of our dream, Raien's and mine."

Again they rode a bit without speaking, and again it was Macurdy who broke the silence, still in a monotone. "Do you love me, Varia?"

"I'll always love you, Curtis. You were my first love, and it changed me more than you can imagine. It showed me what love is, and that I could love. And later it made me strong."

Her cat eyes searched him in the night, so much less dark to her than to him. "I'll always love you, but—I've changed. My dream has changed."

It was Cyncaidh who broke the next silence. "We've heard tales of the amazing General Macurdy. That you ride a wild boar; that you have two rows of teeth—that an Ozian spear maiden loves you, and you've refused her."

Macurdy laughed, a laugh amused but without joy. "I got my front teeth all broken or knocked out back in Oz, and new ones grew in. A whole new set, all nice and straight. They even pushed out the good ones I already had. I never had sprouted wisdom teeth before; I guess that tells you something." He turned to Varia. "I guess it took, when you spelled me to not get old. I guess that's how I grew them. And there is a spear maiden; you're not the only one who knows about loving two at a time." He paused. "You don't suppose you could do for her what you did for me, do you? Give her long youth?"

Varia's teeth gnawed her lower lip thoughtfully. "If she has the necessary ylvin genes. The blood. But that's very unlikely, for someone from Oz. Where is she now?"

"In camp, in the hospital. Someone put a big dent in her helmet, in the battle. She'll be all right though."

"If you can bring her here to me—"

While the two of them discussed the possibilities, Cyncaidh rode quietly, thinking. The commander of the southern army still showed a little of the farmboy Varia had told him about. Had described to him at length, till she'd become comfortable with her memories. He'd come to feel he knew Curtis Macurdy.

Actually he hadn't, and neither had Varia. Or no, that wasn't right: she'd known him as he had been. Then, held to the fire, instead of flaring and dying, or softening, or going brittle, he'd tempered, strengthened, grown into something uncanny, a man who still hadn't learned how powerful he was.

Varia's voice drew him from his reverie. "Raien," she said, "I want to go back with Curtis tomorrow to visit his spear maiden, with a guard platoon to bring me home. I'll only be gone a day."

For just a moment Cyncaidh felt misgiving, but it faded. He—he and A'duaill and Mariil—had come to know her as deeply as you could know anyone, and there was no dishonesty in her. She would come back. And if somehow she changed her mind, what right would he have to complain?

She'd come back though. As she sat in the saddle looking at him, her love assured him of it.

* * *

They started back to camp, and Cyncaidh's thoughts reached ahead to Duinarog. Paedhrig would sign, beyond a doubt, and the agreement with the Rude Lands would be law. Then they'd have to weather the resulting storm. The Expansion Party would be enraged at the agreement, but with Quaie dead there'd be a period, no doubt all too brief, of confusion, probably indecision, and perhaps even conflict within its ranks. Then someone would establish leadership and attempt to drum up public outrage at a treaty without vengeance, made when the smoke of funeral pyres had hardly dissipated.

They'd deal with it, though, he and Paedrigh. If it got bad enough, he'd resign as chief counselor, claiming family reasons, and Paedhrig could appoint Gavriel, a smoother politician. It might be just as well. It might be time for a healer in the Chief Counselor's office. Then, after a time, Paedhrig might appoint him Minister of Southern Affairs.

He smiled to himself. He could stand being dismissed. He'd take Varia back to Aaerodh Manor, and they'd spend a year exploring. Do the coast and islands in his sloop, the rivers by canoe and the forests on skis.

* * *

That night Macurdy lay awake thinking. Last night he'd told Melody he'd marry her, and had wondered how he could have said it. Now he'd learned Varia was married to someone else. Yesterday it had seemed he'd been a fool to imagine this invasion producing anything but disaster and death, and tonight he had an agreement, or seemed to.

It wasn't, he thought, as if things had been preordained. More like, if he just kept doing what seemed right, more good than bad would come of it.

And what about all the dead. What of them?

What indeed? Everyone died sooner or later. Even Sarkia would. And people here believed that after a period in something like purgatory, reviewing what they'd done in life and suffering for their misdeeds, they'd be reborn, until finally they were fit for heaven. It sounded more just than what he'd learned in the Oak Creek Presbyterian Church, though Reverend Fleming wouldn't much approve of it.

He went to sleep on that.

PART 6: *Melody*

Chapter 39: Korens Manor

The next day, riding south with their escorts, Varia and Curtis talked at length, speaking American for privacy. She learned much about his odyssey, and he gained a much better picture of the empire.

Not that they talked continuously. The day was clear but breezy, and cool for Six-Month—ideal for riding and enjoying the countryside—and there were moments of looking about, soaking up perceptions. Once, far overhead, an eagle screamed, and for a time, seven vultures, black as crows, sailed in silent, effortless circles. While the marsh, when they reached it, drew the eyes. It stretched beyond the edge of vision—expanses of cattails, black pools sheened with limonite, and here and there patches of ten-foot reeds, or islands of brush and trees. Creeks the color of tea passed with imperceptible currents beneath stone bridges, while along their narrow back channels, muskrat lodges humped like miniature beaver dens.

For Varia there were moments of reflection. Curtis had just told her of Arbel and his system of training, which obviously had had powerful effects. Yet he was still Curtis, Curtis transformed, much more powerful and charismatic now. Curtis minus much of the imprinting laid on him by family, church, and community, that had prepared him for life in Washington County. Before she'd slept, the night before, Raien had murmured, in reflections of his own, "We met a true lion today, Varia, the Lion of Farside. And discovered a friend."

The Lion of Farside. The metaphor had its attraction, but Curtis wasn't normally ferocious, certainly not cold-blooded. Deadly perhaps, and powerful, but not cold-blooded.

* * *

When they left the marsh behind, Varia was telling him of the irrepressible Hermiss, who lived at Ternass, and the stories she'd told her of life on Farside.

"Hmh! I wonder if she made the connection between your Macurdy and the marshal of the southern army."

"I doubt it. I don't think I mentioned your last name; to me you've always been Curtis, and Will was Will. Sisters and ylver are like most Rude Landers about names: mostly we use just one, however many you have."

The road topped a low hill, and now Varia could see, ahead and to her left, large ovals of ashes. Soldiers raked them, finding and piling bones, while prisoner details dug pits. This, she realized, was the battlefield, where the pyres had burned and the bones would be buried. Raien would be glad to know these things were being done.

They left the road, angling toward the broad tent camp of the southern army, a mile or so ahead. In the fields, whole cohorts played ball, a hundred in each game, or each melee. She wondered how many bones would be broken before the day was over.

Approaching camp, they sent their escorts off to the Kullvordi tentment. Her ylver would be fed there, and have tents assigned them. Then Macurdy led her to his headquarters tentment. As they approached Melody's tent, Varia felt curiosity, and a certain tension. "I hear her talking," Macurdy murmured, still in American, and halted his horse outside. He helped Varia down, though she didn't need help, and led her in as the two women inside looked up.

Varia stared startled, for one of the women was Hermiss, who stared back with her mouth open. "Varia!" she squealed, and rushing to her, hugged her hard, then stepped back to arm's length. "Oh Varia! You're so *beautiful!* As beautiful as ever.

More, with your hair grown out! Where have you *been?* It's so *wonderful* to see you!"

Macurdy watched quizzically, and spoke in Yuultal. "If I had to guess, I'd say you two know each other."

"This is Hermiss that I told you about. My friend on the ride north."

"Ah! Maybe you two ought to go off and talk for an hour or so." He looked at Melody. "If it's all right with you? You and I have things to talk about, too." Melody nodded, frowning more from uncertainty and worry than hostility.

Varia and Hermiss went out into the sun, where Hermiss's horse was picketed too. They mounted, and rode northwest half a mile to a low hill. On the top, they remained in the saddle, watching the breeze riffle the grasses and wildflowers. "What were you doing in Colonel Melody's tent?" Varia asked.

The girl sobered at once. "I...Do you remember when I wondered what it would be like to be raped? I found out. Two nights ago. Some soldiers, Kormehri, came into town and grabbed fifteen of us, and took us to their camp." No longer animated, she described the ordeal. "But we were lucky, otherwise I might be dead now. Only three or four did it to me before Marshal Macurdy came and stopped them. All by himself in the middle of all those horny Kormehri with their breeches off! And when the Kormehri captain wouldn't obey him, Marshal Macurdy killed him with his sword! Then another officer wouldn't either, and he killed him too, and made the soldiers form ranks, and marched them off without their breeches."

She giggled with tension and the image, then hiccuped. Varia could see her quivering. "And do you know what? When he killed the second officer, there was a glowing light on the end of his sword! Some of the other girls saw it too. Then another officer took us to the Sisters, and they gave us pallets, and did magic to heal us and keep us from getting pregnant, and talked to us for quite awhile, asking us questions that seemed to help. And they gave us some of their clothes to wear, because ours were mostly torn and trampled on, and some of Marshal Macurdy's guardsmen took us home.

"And today he rides into camp with you!" Hermiss's normal animation began to return. "How did that happen?"

"A peace was signed this morning, between him and General Cyncaidh. The fighting's over."

"General Cyncaidh?!"

"He's Emperor Paedhrig's chief counselor."

"Really? That's wonderful! And—why did you come here? With Marshal Macurdy?"

The truth wasn't something Varia felt free to share. And if she started, she'd have an involved half hour of explaining to do. So she simply said, "Colonel Melody was hurt in the battle, and might have died. I've come to be sure she's all right. She's quite important to Marshal Macurdy." Varia changed the subject then. "What were you doing in her tent?"

"She talked to all of us who were raped, and gave us money taken from the soldiers who'd been there. To make up for it, or try to. She told us the marshal had had men hanged for raping women, but it still happened sometimes. Marshal Macurdy's really handsome—well, not handsome exactly, but good-looking—and so manly! I'd like to marry him! Not really of course. I'd be scared to death, he's so—*powerful!* Colonel Melody is powerful too, but...I mean, she's probably no older than me, or not very much, but she's a high officer in the southern army! Anyway I stayed around to talk to her more. You know me!"

My God, Hermiss! You're amazing! How long ago was it? Two or three days? And look at you, chattering and full of life! It must have helped, Varia told herself, to have been rescued and seen punishment delivered.

"I asked you some thoughtless questions, before," Hermiss went on, "and I hope this isn't another one. But—what have you been doing, Varia?"

Varia smiled at her. "I'm married, Hermiss. To General Cyncaidh. He's a very nice man—or ylf—thoughtful and loving. And we have a baby boy we've named Ceonigh. The ylver give their children names from their ancient language. Ceonigh means honor, and it sounds lovely, too."

Hermiss threw her arms around Varia, laughing delightedly

and crying at the same time, tears flowing down her cheeks. "Oh Varia," she said, "I'm so happy for you! So *happy!* You *deserve* to have good things. You *deserve* them!"

They talked a little longer, of Duinarog, the Northern Sea, and Aaerodh Manor, then rode back to camp. >From there, Varia, with an escort, accompanied Hermiss home. And when they parted, Varia told herself this time she would surely write to her.

* * *

Varia rode directly back to Melody, whom she found alone. Macurdy had left, to give orders regarding the withdrawal, he'd said. Melody's aura was darkened by jealousy, but showed only a slight residual effect of her concussion, an effect she didn't feel and should be gone in another day. It also showed the usual hint of talent, but when Varia asked questions that should bring any latency to view, she found little. Even so, she decided to carry out the procedure as she had with Will, who'd actually shown more potential. It could do no harm, and if somehow it worked…

Melody was examining Varia as thoroughly as Varia had her. Mostly she saw physical beauty and poise, but her intelligence and power were also obvious. "Why did you come here," Melody asked, "if you're not married to Macurdy anymore? And why are you talking to me?"

Varia considered telling her, then didn't. Macurdy would, if he wanted her to know. Meanwhile she lied. "He asked me to make sure your head injury doesn't give you trouble in the future. But I'll need to put a spell on you."

Melody shook her head with no sign of a wince. "I'll be all right. I don't want anyone putting a spell on me."

"I understand that. I'd feel the same if I were you. Will you allow it when Curtis comes back? If he sits with us?"

Melody pursed her lips, her eyes intent on the Sister. "If he's here, yes. If he wants me to. It's not that I think you'd do something bad. I just don't like the idea."

Varia smiled. *Thank you, spear maiden,* she thought, *for the polite lie. I don't blame you for distrusting me.* "Fine. When he's free, I'll come back with him."

Half an hour later she did. With Macurdy there, it took only two or three minutes to relax Melody sufficiently, four or five more to put her under, and another fifteen or twenty to run the procedure. Then, on a slow count, Varia brought her back to consciousness. After directing her attention to objects in the tent, to reorient her, she asked how she felt.

"All right," Melody said slowly, as if examining how, in fact, she did feel. Then, "I feel fine," and looked at Macurdy as if uncertain what was next.

He grinned at her. "Good. The army will start south the day after tomorrow. The last cohorts will leave two days later. Jeremid will take care of the planning and coordination."

Melody looked bothered by that. "I'm your chief of staff!" she said. "That's my job!"

"Uhm. Actually I had something more important in mind for you. I thought you and I could get married tomorrow afternoon. Jeremid and Tarlok will witness it, and Asperel. I claimed half a helmetful of silver coins from a Teklan plunder wagon, and rented the house of the district governor for two days and nights. The cook and servants come with it. The governor and his wife will stay in town with their son."

Melody had listened, staring. Now, with a whoop, she leaped from the chair and embraced Macurdy, kissing him hard. Varia left without a word.

"Come back after dark tonight, Macurdy," Melody growled, "and they'll have to help you to the wedding. Loro can sleep with the Sisters if she wants to."

Macurdy laughed, disentangling himself from her arms. "Omara wants you to rest till tomorrow, and there's a lot I need to get done so I can give you my full attention after the wedding. I don't want Jeremid interrupting us with a bunch of questions and authorizations to handle."

She made a face at him. "All right, troll prince, one more day. One more day and you're mine." Her next kiss was less forceful and more sensual; he left grinning.

* * *

Varia mused in her tent, feeling vaguely jealous. Not like

an exlover, but more like—a mother! *How dare that impetuous young woman lust for my Curtis!* she asked herself, and chuckled. *Have you forgotten when you seduced him? What a night! It's a good thing his spear maiden's strong; she may get more than she expects.*

Remembering brought a backwash of that lust, but it had little force. Tomorrow morning Curtis would come to say goodbye; they'd shake hands and probably never see one another again. Then she'd ride away north to Raien, not having to wonder any longer, and in a few days they'd be back with baby Ceonigh.

* * *

The house, known locally as Korens Manor, was not large for a governor's residence, but it was more than large enough for Macurdy's two-day honeymoon. He'd chosen the master bedroom suite at one end of the second floor, while his orderly and couriers, and two squads of guards under a lieutenant and two sergeants, occupied rooms on the ground floor. It would have felt unsafe to be there with no more than the servants.

The household staff stayed mostly out of sight. Macurdy and Melody, with the witnesses as their supper guests, were met at the door by the steward, who did his best to ignore the foreign soldiers standing guard with swords and spears. What might they do to him if something happened to their commander? Suppose a piece of meat stuck in his throat! Or some dish upset his stomach and they suspected poison!

Unlikely, he told himself, but wasn't entirely assured. After all, these people were barbarians.

* * *

Macurdy savored the last of his pudding and laid down his spoon. Excellent, he told himself, especially considering civilian distribution of everything, food in particular, had been disrupted by his foraging parties. The wine, the first he'd ever drunk, had even been cool.

"Here's to the cook!" Jeremid said cheerfully, pushing back his chair.

"Here's what to the cook?" Macurdy countered. "We need

to take a collection for her. And for the steward; he's probably the one who actually got the stuff."

"The locals will be glad to see us go," Tarlok grunted. "They're on edge. Been holding their breath, afraid we'll go on a rampage before we leave. You can almost smell it when you deal with them."

Macurdy turned his gaze to Jeremid. "I'm depending on our operations officer to see no one does."

Jeremid grinned. "I've got ears out to here." He gestured, indicating something rabbit-like. "But it's unlikely. The whole army heard what you did, or supposedly did, in the Kormehri camp. Not that the Kormehri exaggerated." He laughed. "Not having been there, I get this picture of you buffaloing a whole damn company all by yourself, pulling guys off women by the hair, gutting the company commander and first sergeant, and marching the rest of them out to the battlefield bare-assed, then running them in circles till their balls dragged."

Tarlok snorted. "Ozman, I *was* there. Not that I did anything to help; I was scared spitless. And what you just said is a pretty good description. If I'd tried it, or you, or both of us together, they'd have torn us apart. And if we'd gone in with a company of guards, there'd have been a riot as bad as the damned battle."

"That's the secret," Macurdy said. "Do it alone. Grab guys and start yanking them around. They don't know what to do then; they think you must be more than you are."

Tarlok shook his head. "If it'd been me, they'd have carved me up like a solstice ox. Besides, I saw your sword when you…"

Melody had been watching and listening without taking part. Now, getting to her feet, she interrupted. Firmly. "That's it! Party's over! The good guest knows when to leave, and this is when. I'm taking my husband upstairs and scrub his back for him."

"Spear maiden…" Jeremid began, then thought better of it. "May it be a night to remember. Macurdy, I'm glad you finally got smart. You two belong together."

Melody left then, while Macurdy walked their guests to the front door and out onto the lawn, where he shook hands with the three of them: Jeremid, Tarlok, and the Teklan, Asperel, who'd felt a little out of place with these exrebel comrades. They waited without saying a lot, while their orderlies saddled and brought their horses. Then Macurdy watched them ride off in the dusk before going inside and up to his suite.

He'd half expected Melody to be waiting naked, but she fooled him. She'd undressed, but put on a robe found in a closet. And with the robe, a serious face.

"Did I tell you you're beautiful, spear maiden?" he asked quietly.

"No, but I knew it anyway. Pretty, at least."

"Did I tell you I've been looking forward to this?"

Her gaze was searching. "Have you really?"

He stepped to her, put his arms around her inside her robe, and pulling her close, kissed her, then kissed her again before stepping back.

"Take your clothes off, Macurdy," she said quietly. "Unless you'd rather I did it for you."

He took them off himself while she watched. When he was naked, she dropped her robe. "Do you know what, Macurdy?"

He stared. "What, Melody?" He'd have to stop calling her spear maiden, he decided. She was too beautiful.

"I'm nervous," she said quietly. "I can't believe it, but I'm nervous. And the bath is hot. Hot enough I closed the flue from the stove."

He took her hand. "Then let's go try it out."

They walked into the small adjacent bath. The tub was tiled and half sunken, big enough for four or five to sit. The water wasn't as hot as he'd expected, but more than warm enough, given it was Six-Month and the room warmed by the stove. They sat not across from each other, but side by side, and within seconds were kissing again, embracing, fondling. Without either suggesting it, they got to their feet and clambered dripping from the tub. Towels had been set out on a bench, and they dried hurriedly, then went into the bedroom.

* * *

Later they donned robes and stepped out onto a balcony that

overlooked fields. Dusk had thickened into twilight, and twilight into night, with the crescent moon still well up in the west. There was a cushioned bench, and they sat down on it together, for some time simply holding hands, saying nothing. At length Melody turned and found him looking at her. "I love you, Macurdy," she murmured. "I really do. I have all along, but now it's different. You're a marvelous lover. I thought you'd probably be rough the first time, like a stallion, you're so damned big and strong. And that would have been fine. But you're not. You're thoughtful and loving, and you do the right thing at the right time. It was nicer than I'd ever imagined."

She leaned and kissed him. "This is going to last a long time," she murmured. They kissed some more, and her hand slipped inside his robe. A minute later they went back inside.

* * *

Private Olvi Kalister stood on the porch beside the front entrance, spear butted by his right foot, thoughts on what he imagined was going on inside. He had a wife back at North Fork, whom he hadn't seen now for—he didn't pay much attention to dates, but it seemed like a long time. A mosquito hummed beside his face, then touched down on his cheek, and absently he crushed it.

"Did you get him?" Private Malakum murmured.

"If I didn't, I scared shit out of him."

"I'll bet they're not paying any attention to mosquitoes upstairs."

"I've heard mosquitoes don't bite Macurdy. Flies either, or cooties."

I'll bet right now they could bite his bobbing ass twenty at a time, Malakum told himself, *and he'd never notice.* "You hear all kinds of things," he said.

"I heard when he went in and yanked the Kormehri around the other night, there was a ball of fire on the point of his saber."

Malakum said nothing; he tended to skepticism. On the other hand, Macurdy'd done some uncanny stuff, in front of people Malakum knew well.

The door opened between the two men, and Corporal Freck

stepped out. "You guys thirsty?" he asked in a half whisper.

The sentries' attention sharpened. "What have you got in mind?"

The corporal chuckled. "A couple of us were snooping around the basement with a torch. Found a trapdoor in the floor, and went down in." He held out a small jug. "It's where they store their ale. We figured if the bigwigs could have a party, we ought to have one too. A little one, not enough to get drunk and in trouble. To celebrate the wedding. And the war being over without us getting killed; now there's a reason! This one's yours." He handed it to Malakum. "The stopper's out—didn't want it lying on the porch in the morning—but no one's drunk out of it yet. Just keep quiet, and bring the jug with you when you're relieved."

He went back in and closed the door softly behind him. Malakum took a swig, exhaled a forcible "Ah!" and handed the bottle to Olvi. "Good stuff," he said. "Strong."

Olvi drank and grunted. "Better than my Uncle Loth brews. Freck is all right, bringing us this." They continued passing it back and forth, and after a bit sat down on the top step, their spears lying beside them. Olvi had been part of Orthal's Company when Macurdy first turned up, and without exaggerating much, told stories about their commander. By the time the jug was empty, each man had relieved his bladder onto a shrub, and the moon had set.

Then a woman's scream tore the air, from inside, and both guards jumped to their feet, spears in hand, unsure where it had come from, though it almost had to be...It was followed almost at once by a roar of anger, also inside, and a moment later another, this time from the balcony outside the marshal's suite.

"Get beneath the balcony!" Malakum snapped, then banged through the door, headed for the stairs, and bounded up three at a time. From the far wing, boots hammered down the hall, for the windows were open, and the screams had reached the guardroom. At the last door on his left, he grabbed the handle, turned it and yanked, then dashed in. The only light came from the corridor, enough to see dimly a large figure half dragging and half carrying a smaller, who was struggling and swearing. The marshal's voice shouted, "Bring a lamp, for God's sake!" and Malakum sprinted back out to take one from a tripod in the hall. By that time two more guardsmen came dashing up, one of them barefoot, and ran in.

The marshal stood naked, one thick arm across the throat of a man fully dressed. Blood ran down the marshal's right forearm, and both men were smeared with it. The bed was overturned, the mattress partly beside and partly beneath it. "Get manacles," he said, his voice controlled now. "And turn the bed over. I think Colonel Melody's under the mattress."

Malakum, holding the lamp, stared while the barefoot guard upended the bed onto its feet and threw the mattress on it. On the floor was the marshal's naked bride, bloody from face to feet, either dead or unconscious. More men came in. Malakum looked back at the marshal. The officer of the guard tried to manacle the intruder, and when he resisted, the marshal's arm tightened against the attacker's throat till he went slack.

As soon as the man was shackled, the marshal moved to his wife, swept the sheet off the bed and threw it to a guard. "Make bandages!" he snapped, and the guard began to tear it into broad strips. The marshal's hands went to two of his bride's worst knife wounds, and he began to chant. After a minute he turned to the guardsmen, his voice level but intense. "Send someone to the Sisters. Fast! Tell Sister Omara what's happened, and bring her right away. And take that—" he gestured with his head at the prisoner "—outside. But don't damage him. I'll do the damaging myself, later."

Then he turned back to his bride as if none of them were there, continuing to touch and chant while Private Malakum stood wooden with dismay.

* * *

Lieutenant Sarsli and one of the guards took the intruder out between them, the man's feet bumping down the stairs. "Be glad it's not your head," the guard said. Macurdy had dislocated the man's elbow, and the soldier jerked the arm a couple of times, making the man cry out in pain. "Stop that!" Sarsli snapped.

"You heard what the marshal said." They hustled the prisoner out the front door and onto the lawn, where the soldier threw him down.

"How did you get in there?" Sarsli demanded.

"How do you suppose?" The man's voice was high-pitched with emotion. "I climbed the vines to the balcony. And I'd have killed him, if it hadn't been so damned dark in there. I stabbed his whore by mistake."

"The vines?" Sarsli turned and stared at Olvi, who'd come back to the porch.

The intruder laughed bitterly. "I watched from the fence while your so-called guards sat drinking and talking on the porch. When the moon went down, I sneaked across the lawn and climbed the vines. They wouldn't have noticed if I'd gone over and goosed them."

Oh shit! Sarsli thought, dread settling in his gut. He'd known about the ale. He should have made sure the men on watch didn't get any. No one should have; he should have stashed it till they went back to camp. The marshal would likely kill him now; flogging wouldn't be enough. For just a moment Sarsli considered killing the prisoner, but that wouldn't help. The marshal would find out about the ale anyway, and have two reasons to kill him. As it was, he might be lucky, and a flogging he could survive. Especially, he told himself, when he so richly deserved it.

* * *

Macurdy sat naked and bloody on the bed beside his bride. She had an aura, but he could find no pulse. He'd had one of the guards light the lamps in the room, and bring him wet cloths. Arbel's blood-stopping spell had worked, and now, gently but firmly, he washed the congealing blood from around the multiple stab wounds on her breasts and left shoulder, the deep and ugly slash on her left arm. But didn't bandage them; when Omara came, she'd want to see them.

He became aware the soldier who'd brought in the first lamp still stood holding it. "Soldier," he said softly, "didn't I say everyone out?"

"Yessir."

He watched the man's aura flicker. "What is it you want to tell me?"

"Marshal Macurdy, sir, I was on guard at the front door. I'm to blame for what happened. For that guy getting in."

"I doubt he came in the front door."

"No sir, I'm sure he didn't. Nor any other door. The lieutenant locked them before I ever came on watch, and posted a guard at each end of the downstairs hall. He must have climbed the vines to the balcony. We should have seen him from the porch, crossing the grass, but we had a jug of ale, and sat there talking and forgot to watch. We weren't drunk. We were just—" he paused, swallowed—"celebrating your wedding."

Macurdy looked at him silently for a moment, and when he spoke, it was quietly. "It's done now. We'll see later what we need to do about that."

"Yessir."

"Take the lamp back where you got it and tell my orderly and couriers to stay where they are in case I need them. They're out in the hall, not sure what to do. Then go back to your post."

"Yessir." The man left.

Jesus Christ, Macurdy thought, *celebrating my wedding,* then began the healing formulas Arbel had taught him for loss of blood.

* * *

He couldn't have said how much time had passed when Omara entered with her aide. He'd heard them coming down the hall, along with someone wearing boots, but only the Sisters came in. Omara's eyes settled on Melody. "Wash yourself, Marshal," she said. "I'll see to her."

Going to the washstand at one side of the room, he filled the basin and washed, while behind him, Omara half sang, half murmured her spells. Most of the blood that reddened the wash water was Melody's, he decided. The knife gash on his arm seemed to have stopped bleeding by itself, though it was deep enough that tonus kept it open. He wondered if Varia's spell of long youth had made a difference.

When he'd washed, he pulled on a pair of breeches, then

went back to watch Omara work. The Sister looked up at him. "She'll live," she said, examining him calmly. "Who taught you healing? Varia?"

"We weren't together long enough. I learned it from a shaman in Oz. I was his student for a while, but did poorly on my healing tests."

"It wasn't for lack of talent." Omara turned to her aide. "Narella, bandage her. Tightly so the healing spells work properly. We don't want great scars on the marshal's bride."

She got up from the bed, a handsome woman in uniform, managing to seem long mature, despite her youthful appearance. Macurdy wondered how old she actually was. "Let me bandage your forearm, Macurdy," she said. "Gaping like that, the scar will be large and subject to damage. Besides, the blood needs to circulate through the flesh there."

After she'd washed and bandaged it, she sang a brief formula quite different from Arbel's. When she was done, she stepped back and looked at him. "I'll stay with her tonight. Wounds and blood loss like hers shock deeply. I'll not harm her, nor anyone in my care. I was trained first in healing, and only later in other magicks."

Her aura assured him. "Thank you," he said. "I have to see about something." He finished dressing, donned boots, then belted on his knife and saber, and left. On the lawn, a whole platoon of soldiers were guarding Melody's attacker now, despite his manacles. They'd been sent for, as if Sarsli thought someone might try to rescue the man.

Macurdy stopped a few feet away and stared at the attacker. A youth, really, staring back gray-faced but defiant. "Stand him on his feet," Macurdy said. Two soldiers lifted the young man by the arms so that he cried out with pain. When he was standing, Macurdy drew his knife.

"My wife will live. She won't even be badly scarred. Does that cheer you?"

"It wasn't her I climbed the vines to kill. It was you! And if it hadn't been so dark...But if killing her would hurt you enough, I could still rejoice in it."

"And you like knives. Have you ever been cut by one? Badly?"

The man said nothing, but fear collapsed his aura.

"I'll show you what it's like. First I'll cut off your ears, then your nose, then your horn and balls, and then…"

Abruptly words burst from the young man. "And what of my father? Will you let him do those things to you? A squad of your soldiers raped my mother and sister in front of him, and laughed when he wept and pleaded with them. They took my sister with them when they left with our valuables; God knows what became of her. Afterward my mother killed herself. Will you let him cut you up for that?"

Macurdy stared a long moment. "Where did this happen?"

"In the village of Black Gum, some ninety miles south. My father is the miller there."

"How did you know where to find me?"

For a moment it seemed the youth might refuse to say more; then he answered. "I'd been here in Ternass, apprenticing as a teacher in the common school. When I heard your army had crossed the river, I went home. Too late. So I came back to avenge my family." His defiance faded, leaving him momentarily desolate, but he rallied. "When I got here, everyone was talking about your wedding, as if it was something to celebrate! Everyone knew where you'd be staying. And we apprentices had been invited to the governor's once for Learning Day. Given a tour. I could guess what room you'd be in."

"Um." Macurdy sheathed his knife. "The people in Ternass had something bigger than a wedding to celebrate. A peace has been signed."

"Peace! What good is peace to my family?"

Instead of answering, Macurdy turned to his orderly. "Bring my horse. And one for the prisoner."

* * *

With three soldiers, Macurdy took the youth into Ternass, to the jail there, and had the jailer wakened. The man went pale at Macurdy's story. "We'll…we'll have him tried tomorrow, I'm sure. And hanged promptly."

"No. I want no trial or hanging. Lock him up. Have a physician do something for his elbow. Keep him here for a week before you let him go. And while he's here, have him visited by the girls I rescued. His soul is scarred like my wife's body. Perhaps their stories will help him." He paused. "There's one named Hermiss I met two days ago. A friend of the Cyncaidh's wife. Let her arrange it."

"Hermiss? I know her! Her father is principal of the common school."

Macurdy's eyes widened for a moment. "She'll be perfect. No doubt she knows this young man."

* * *

As he rode back to the manor, Macurdy told himself grimly that if this had to happen, some good would come of it yet.

Chapter 40: Squire Macurdy

Even with frequent healing attention by Omara, and by Macurdy as his skill improved, it was the fifth day after the attack before Melody was strong enough to travel safely and with reasonable comfort. (On the other hand, a physician from Farside would have disbelieved the rate of healing—been impressed she'd even survived. Not only had blood loss been heavy; her right pleura had been punctured, and the lung collapsed.) By the time they left, the last cohorts were gone, except for their escort, the Kullvordi 2nd Cavalry.

Keeping an easy pace, they reached the Big River after the last infantry cohorts had been ferried across. And traveling more briskly, reached Teklapori eight days later, with Melody fully recovered.

Travel stained, they were ushered into the palace. Inside it had changed conspicuously, the old hangings and furniture mostly replaced. Even Macurdy noticed. It was lighter and brighter, less ornate, less of a hodgepodge. Within minutes a servant came to tell them King Pavo was waiting for them in the guest parlor. "Two men were with him on business of the crown," the servant added, "but he has sent them away for now." Then he bowed again and gestured them to follow.

They found Wollerda in uniform, one Macurdy hadn't seen before. The design was the same—the elegantly simple Sisterhood guardsman design—but the material had a velvety sheen, while over one shoulder was a sash that looked to Macurdy like silk, with alternating stripes of Teklan red and Kullvordi blue. He wore a crown, though not the bejewelled ceremonial crown, and beneath it all, he'd gained weight.

Wollerda was grinning from ear to ear as he stepped quickly to meet them halfway to the throne: Queen Liiset remained in the background as the two exrebels gripped and shook hands. "It's good to have you back," Wollerda said, then looked at Melody. "And you, Colonel. Your husband reported your injuries, both in battle and later."

When he'd seated them, he fixed Macurdy with his gaze. "What did you do to her attacker? You didn't say."

Macurdy told him, the story bringing a gradient raising of the royal eyebrows. When it was done, Wollerda looked at Melody. "What do you think of that?"

She shrugged. "He's the commander. And when he explained it...The man acted in hatred, for a reason; I'd have done the same, except I wouldn't have botched it. And the story will have spread—he may even have taken it home himself—spread like the story of how Macurdy handled the rapes at Ternass. It'll give the Rude Lands, maybe even the empire, a different view of us here."

Wollerda's lips pursed, and he looked at Macurdy. "You reported some hangings earlier. What happened at Ternass?"

Macurdy told that one, too, leaving out only the ball of glowing plasma at the end of his saber, chuckling now at the memory of the Kormehri running bare-assed.

Wollerda's eyebrows had returned to the rest position. "Macurdy," he said, "I've seen wisdom from you before, but that was true genius." He turned to Liiset. "Show the colonel the changes you've made here. The marshal and I are going to talk about his negotiations with Cyncaidh. I'll send word when we're done."

"Of course, Your Majesty," Liiset answered, and smiling at Melody, led her from the room. Melody would rather have stayed, but didn't argue. When they were gone, Wollerda grinned again.

"Actually I want to talk about more personal matters: about your Varia and my Liiset. Since I married Liiset, I've looked differently at the Sisterhood. And I also understand why you were so determined to recover your Varia. Her twin is a wonderful wife, whether we're at the table discussing matters of state, or in bed." He grinned. "And she never demands." His grin skewed a bit. "But then, she hardly needs to. Her wishes are seldom far from my own, seldom far enough to refuse. I suspect she sometimes judges how far I can be moved, and sets her comments and suggestions accordingly." He chuckled drily. "I've learned a lot from her; there are things I look at quite differently now than I did."

He eyed Macurdy shrewdly. "You wonder if that's good, eh? All in all it is. Before, my opinions were too fixed, my ideals sometimes at odds with good sense; the Sisters have things to teach us. Not Sarkia's ready ruthlessness, but…"

He changed the subject. "Your reports said nothing about getting your Varia back, only that you'd married Melody. What happened?"

Macurdy looked at his palms as if something were written on them. "She was there: Varia, with Cyncaidh. She's his wife."

"Ah." Wollerda peered intently at Macurdy. "I'd like to know more about that. There may be insights there."

Macurdy shrugged, then summarized her odyssey from escaping the Cloister to arriving at Aaeroth Manor. "And when Cyncaidh got her home—he told me this—he and his wife, who was far gone in decline and died soon afterward, worked on her until she agreed to marry him. Told her she didn't have a chance of ever getting to me again. He said they lied to her to break her down. *Exaggerated* is the word he used."

Neither man said anything more for a minute, then Wollerda asked another question. "You wrote that Quaie was dead, you killed him yourself. How did *that* happen?"

Macurdy told him. Wollerda stared. "A ball of fire? That's a magic I never heard of before." He shook his head. "But you've got something beyond magic, Macurdy: beyond it and more important. You've got a knack for doing and saying the right thing. Or maybe that's magic. Anyway, Liiset reported to the Dynast you'd killed Quaie, and—" Wollerda got up and went to a side table—"she sent you a letter we're both curious about.

Wollerda gave a wax-sealed envelope to Macurdy, who

opened it with his dagger and removed the letter. It was brief, and when he'd finished reading, he looked at Wollerda. "She wants me to visit the Cloister. She has an important position for me, if I'm interested."

"Are you?"

Macurdy shook his head. "Nope. I can't even imagine what she might offer."

"It could be better than I can offer," Wollerda pointed out. "In some respects, anyway. You'd have more influence from there than from here."

"There's only one Sister I ever wanted to be around, and that's over now. There are other Sisters I like, since I've gotten to know them. Liiset of course. And Omara, who was in charge of the sorcery unit with the army. She did a lot of good; among other things she saved Melody's life. And I got along with Sarkia all right, when we were negotiating. But..." He shrugged again. "Sarkia's too cold-blooded for me. And the things she had done to Varia—if I'd known about them earlier, I'd have killed her." He exhaled audibly. "I'll send her a message; tell her I plan to stay in Tekalos, to farm and have children."

"Maybe things will change in the Sisterhood," Wollerda said thoughtfully. "When someone else takes over."

Macurdy, seeing the aura as well as the man, looked sharply at him. "What haven't you told me?"

Wollerda shrugged. "Liiset doesn't often say what's in the messages she gets from the Cloister, but...Two weeks ago, when she read one, she got a strange look. And didn't put the letter away as she usually does—as if she intended to read it again first. Then I had a chance and read it myself. Sarkia asked who she'd recommend as the new Dynast, when the time came that one was needed. Asked for four names, and who she'd recommend *not* be considered.

"Later on she said to me, 'You read my message from the Dynast, didn't you?' and I admitted it of course." He looked meaningfully at Macurdy. "I asked Liiset once who she thought would eventually replace Sarkia, and she said that was one thing Sarkia never talked about. So. What caused her to think about it now?" Wollerda paused as if to stress what he said next. "Then, after her last weekly message, Liiset reminded me of that. And said, 'The Dynast has gone into seclusion. She's at the Cloister, but staying in her suite.' " He shrugged. "Looks as if time has finally caught up with her."

Macurdy nodded thoughtfully. "Who did Liiset recommend, do you know?"

Wollerda shook his head. "I'll ask her at supper. She might even tell us."

* * *

At supper, Macurdy got a pretty good idea how Wollerda had gained weight; this wasn't the simple fare he'd eaten as a commander of rebels. When they'd finished, a light wine was served. Macurdy drank buttermilk, instead, and they talked of his plans to farm. He had in mind to try certain Indiana practices in Teklan conditions.

"I had the idea you wanted to be ambassador to the empire," Wollerda said.

Macurdy looked at his wife. "I doubt Melody would like living in a city, especially where people might be hostile to us. She might run someone through before it was over."

"Well, if you're set on farming, I've got a farm for you. Actually a choice of two large estates. Their exowners were guilty of major tax frauds."

"What will the locals think of that? The neighbors around there?"

"They'll cheer. They're smallholders, and both the men I've thrown in prison were old favorites of Gurtho, arrogant and overbearing." He cocked an eyebrow. "Actually I had another job I'd hoped you'd take, if you turned down the ambassadorship. And to tell the truth, I can't imagine you being satisfied as a farmer very long, after what you've been doing."

Macurdy shook his head, laughing. "You don't know me as well as you think. I'm a farmer born and bred." He paused. "What did you have in mind?"

"Minister of Revenue. It needs a strong man, the income is more reliable than farming, and you'd have a lot of influence."

Macurdy shook his head vigorously. "No way in hell would I take that job. You might consider Tarlok though; he could do it, do it right. And Kithro's worth considering as ambassador."

"Hmm. You know, that's a good idea. Both of them are. I'll take it up with them."

"Just don't tell Tarlok I recommended him."

Wollerda grunted. "Anyone who'd want the job, I'd rather not give it to. In running a kingdom, money's a problem, but if you don't tax honestly, the whole thing turns sour."

Macurdy sipped his buttermilk, saying nothing. He was thinking about the new furniture and wall hangings in the palace, all expensive.

Wollerda's next words popped Macurdy out of his reverie. "Liiset," he said, "who did you recommend to the Dynast as dynast-designate? And who did you recommend against? Can you tell us?"

Liiset looked at him calmly. "Of the four I recommended, only two are anyone you know of. My first recommendation was Varia, if we could somehow get her back. When we were young, she was trained for the executive staff. But that's out, since she's married Cyncaidh. And my second—" She turned to their guests. "My second was Curtis Macurdy." They gawped, Macurdy especially. "You're of Sisterhood lineage," she pointed out, "and I see no reason the Dynast has to be a woman, though who knows how Sarkia might look at it. As for recommending against someone—I'll keep that to myself. It's not someone I dislike; simply someone whose appointment would be unfortunate, a source of abrasion and conflict."

Liiset's report introverted them, killing the conversation. After a few minutes, Wollerda excused them.

* * *

Before they went to sleep, Melody lay gazing at the ceiling. "Macurdy," she said, "I'm glad you refused to be the tax collector."

He grunted. "It's a lousy job. A lot of people are going to resent whoever does it, even if he's honest. To do a good job of it, you've got to push, even throw people in jail. If I had to do that, I'd get mad every time I saw money wasted, and any government invented by man is going to waste money. Even if it's only poor judgment."

Melody nodded. "I grew up thinking there were only three honorable professions: soldier, farmer, and shaman. And I'd rather have you be a farmer. Farmers are home at night." She turned on her side, fondled him, felt him swell. "Soldiers are likelier to get killed, too." She raised up on an elbow, kissed him and threw a leg across his. "And I want us to be together a long long time."

* * *

They moved to one of the farms, into a house with eight rooms plus kitchen, pantry, cellar, and servants' wing. The field hands had kept the crops in decent tilth, and Macurdy had no difficulties with any of them. Summer faded into fall, and Melody learned about morning sickness. The corn was harvested, the potatoes dug, and fall plowing gotten under way. Farming wasn't as satisfying as he remembered it, but Macurdy told himself that would change when the crops were crops he'd planted himself. And when he learned where to get alfalfa seed, and peanuts, and other things he wanted to try.

One noon, he came up from the fields to find a large and familiar black bird perched on the roof, looking coldly at the cats, all of them interested but tentative. No doubt partly because of his size, but also because he was scolding them in a perfectly human voice.

"Blue Wing!" Macurdy shouted joyously. "It's great to see you!"

"Really! How great could that possibly be when you keep creatures like those around?"

"The cats? There's not one who'd tackle you. They're not foolish enough for that."

"As long as I don't fall asleep."

Macurdy ran them off—as barn cats they were wary of him anyway—and Blue Wing glided down to the porch roof.

"Where've you been the past year?" Macurdy asked.

"I helped raise a pair of young, and amongst my kind, it

takes till nearly the equinox before they can forage for themselves."

"Did you bring your wife along?"

"By wife I presume you mean a permanent mate. Happily we don't have such aberrated concepts." He eyed Macurdy. "Perhaps for a species like yours, that takes so ridiculously long to mature their young and tends to have more or less permanent residences, an arrangement such as marriage makes sense. But for the more fortunate..."

Macurdy grinned. "I'm married, you know. To Melody."

"I'm aware of that. We have already spoken, she and I. I'm also aware she will give birth next summer. And frankly, I think she'd be much better off laying eggs than in passing something the size of a human infant through her vent. After carrying it around inside her for the better part of a year! Outrageous!"

"How'd you like to stay around this winter? I'll make you a perch in the corner of the windbreak, where the winter winds won't be so bad, and put a roof on it to keep the rain and sleet off. On top of a twelve-foot post, on a platform so the cats can't bother you, or a weasel. And nail a sheet of copper around the post near the top, so they can't get close enough to scrabble at the platform. How about it?"

* * *

Macurdy built the perch that same day, Blue Wing supervising, and although afterward the bird was off roving much of the time, over the weeks before winter they had several good conversations. Through his species' hive mind, the bird had heard quite a bit about the war, but what he learned from Macurdy was both broader and more detailed than any other great raven had learned. And when Macurdy was in the fields working, or in the woods with his men cutting firewood, Blue Wing sometimes accompanied Melody on her almost daily rides, perched on her wrist like a falconer's hawk so they could talk more easily. It was mostly she who fed him, when he was around.

Mostly though she rode alone or with Macurdy. The Green River, broad and dark, formed the south boundary of the estate, and they enjoyed exploring the woods that bordered it, both on the flood plain and the first terrace. Coons were numerous, and possums and fox squirrels. Floods were too extreme for beaver and muskrats, and deer and razorback were scarce because of hunting, but porcupines and otters weren't uncommon. Sometimes they saw tracks of bobcat and fox. And of course, cows that trailed down to drink.

Once Melody called, "Macurdy! Come here! There's something you've got to see!"

He rode over to where she sat in the saddle, pointing at a patch of heavily disturbed ground. Something had been rooting up roots or tubers of some sort; skunk-cabbage he supposed. "Looks like a really big razorback," he said.

She shook her head, led him to the shore, and pointed to an exposed sandy mud flat. "Look at those."

He saw hoof prints, sharp and deep, far bigger than any razorback's he knew of. "I've never seen any before," she said, "and never expected to, certainly not in country as cleared and farmed as this."

Macurdy chewed a lip. A great boar could mean trouble. Something that large could hardly sustain itself on skunk-cabbage; in country without much large game, it would prey on livestock. And while he didn't believe in enchanted swine with powers of witchcraft, even in Yuulith, he could very well believe in an animal so cunning it could be thought of as supernatural. Hopefully it was merely passing through. If it took only a calf or two, he'd call it a bargain.

They found where the tracks moved on, and leaning forward in the saddle, Melody started following them.

"Where are you going?"

"To see if we can come up on it. We'll probably never have another chance to see one."

"Hey! Wait now! They're dangerous!"

She looked at him as if to say, "So?"

"Suppose you do? And suppose he doesn't like it?"

"Then he'd have to run fast enough to catch us."

"He just might do that."

"Damn it, Macurdy! Who's the one that climbed the tree to

chase the jaguar out?"

"I didn't have any choice."

"Well then, who went into the fallen timber and buffaloed Slaney? And who went into the Kormehri camp and fronted down a whole damned company?"

"I *had* to do those things, honey. I didn't have any choice!"

"Macurdy, you can be so exasperating!"

"Besides, you're pregnant. If something happens to you..."

She swore at him, and turning her horse, trotted across the bottomland and up onto the terrace, Macurdy trotting Hog a bit behind. He knew what would happen next, and he was right; when she got onto the firmer high ground, she kicked her horse into a gallop. The last he saw of her, she'd crossed a field of corn stubble and cleared the rail fence on the other side. He shook his head, wondering if she'd ever get over her reckless streak. *After the baby comes,* he told himself. If she didn't jiggle and jar it to death first. He wasn't going to bring that up though. Not again.

To his relief, there was no predation. The great boar passed through the neighborhood leaving no damage behind.

* * *

They had snow cover two weeks before the solstice, which everyone said was early. And when, a month later, it had deepened instead of melting, they said it was the hardest winter they'd ever seen. Finally, in mid-One-Month, a thaw arrived, with an all-night rain that took the snow out at one shot.

Meanwhile Melody had begun to swell, and not long afterward could feel the fetus move inside her. In bed, she'd place Macurdy's hand where he could feel it, and he decided he loved her more than ever. She was more affectionate than ever, too, given to kissing him without warning—or without cause, so far as he could see.

One night after they'd made careful love, she lay gentle fingers on his cheek. "Liiset calls you Curtis," she said. "Is that what Varia called you?"

"Um-hmm."

"Would you like me to call you that?"

"If you'd like. I like whatever you call me." He chuckled.

"Except when you're mad at me. Some of those names I don't like too well."

"Curtis," she said thoughtfully. "Curtis. I like it." She kissed him. "Curtis, I love you. I love you very much."

And when they got up in the morning, she still called him Curtis. She stopped running her horse, too, settling for a walking gait, or an easy trot. *She's settling down,* he told himself. *At last.*

* * *

In the beginning of Two-Month, with the ground bare, the big freeze struck. The fireplaces, never adequate in cold weather, seemed almost useless now. More blankets were piled on the beds, enough they had to wake up to turn over. Ice froze in the pail in the kitchen, and despite the fireplace, burst the ceramic pitcher on the washstand in their bedroom. Macurdy let Blue Wing perch on the mantle in the living room, though the bird suffered from claustrophobia indoors. Then, blowing on his fingers from time to time, the squire of Macurdy Manor sat down and drew plans for a brick stove, with flues to be built in the walls between the living room and the rooms adjacent, intending to build it the next summer.

* * *

The big freeze lasted for four days, cold enough that when he went outside, even at midday, the hairs in his nostrils stiffened. Something which, back home in Washington County, was taken to mean the temperature was below zero.

This time the cold broke without a storm; on the fifth day it simply warmed up. Not up to freezing—not that warm—but the bright sun felt good on his face, and the cows were let out for the exercise. The sparrows and crows were out too, those that hadn't died. And Blue Wing. After five days with only brief hours outside, he flew high and wide. "The river is frozen," he announced when he returned, and said that was something rare for the Green. The ground was certainly frozen—as hard as the new concrete pavement on Main Street back in Salem.

The next day dawned warmer than the day before. Toward noon the temperature rose above freezing, the bright sun shining on a slick of mud atop the frozen ground, and Macurdy and Melody saddled their horses for a ride. The cattle tracks went directly to the pasture above the woods, and when the two riders got there, Macurdy rode around examining what condition it was in, while Melody rode down to see the frozen river, and Blue Wing soared high overhead. The pasture grass was a mixture, and grazed-down enough Macurdy wasn't sure what species dominated. Nor how much winter-kill there might be, given such severe cold without snow cover.

He heard Blue Wing shrieking something and looked up, to see the raven spiraling down, almost diving. The short hairs bristled on Macurdy's neck. Then he discerned the words: "Macurdy! Macurdy! The ice has broken! Melody is in the water!"

Thumping Hog's flanks with his heels, Macurdy galloped as recklessly as Melody ever had. At the river bank he pulled up. The hole was mostly full of broken ice, and only her horse's head showed, whinnying wildly. *She's gone under the ice,* Macurdy thought, and galloped wildly downstream, where eighty yards away he could see water kept open by rapids. If he could get there before she was carried through and under the next ice…

He got there just as she emerged, and Hog didn't hesitate when Macurdy drove him into water shockingly, deathly cold, reaching her near the foot of the rip. Leaning down, he grabbed her sodden coat with a grip of iron, then Hog fought their way across the current back to shore. Macurdy jumped down and examined her; there was no trace of spirit aura; little even of body aura.

He howled then, howled at the sky like a hound. But only once before turning her over on her stomach and beginning the artificial respiration he'd learned in grade school, at the same time chanting brokenly a formula Arbel had taught him. He pressed and relaxed, pressed and relaxed, until, soaked as he was, he was shivering almost too violently to continue. *God!* he prayed silently, *let her live, and I'll do anything you ask!* He knew artificial respiration would be useless if long interrupted, yet feared any life which might remain would freeze out of her, so after half an hour, his hands and mind numbed by cold and shock, he stopped. High clouds had moved in to block the sun, as if God himself had turned against him.

Almost too cold to function, he struggled the dead body across Hog's shoulders, then managed, barely, to pull himself into the saddle. At the house, he carried what had been Melody into the living room, while his houseman, who'd come into the room to investigate, melted back out in shock. There was no trace of aura now. He stripped her, dried her, wrapped her in blankets, and laid her out in front of the fireplace. Then, long after there was any use in it, he began artificial respiration again. He had only a vague notion of time, but finally was aware her body was stiffening.

Moving woodenly, he carried her into the bedroom, washed her, painstakingly brushed her hair, and got her into clean clothes—her dress uniform, stored in a cedar chest against moths. When that was done, he called for his houseman, who came in wide-eyed and silent.

"Have Dellerd harness Socks and hitch him to the buggy. I'm taking my wife to Teklapori."

Not trusting his voice, the houseman nodded silently and disappeared. When he was gone, Macurdy wept violently for about a minute—hard racking sobs that shook his whole body, while the tears sluiced. Then it passed. Stripping himself before the bedroom fire, he rubbed his body with a rough towel till he was red and tingling with renewed circulation. That done, he dressed in dry clothes, put on a heavy coat, and carried the body out to the buggy—a sort of surrey with the back enclosed—where he lay it gently on the back seat. Then, after giving a few instructions to the houseman and farm foreman, he drove off down the road toward the capital, a silent Blue Wing flying low overhead.

PART 7: Goodbyes

Chapter 41: Farewell to Melody

I took it easy, driving in to Teklapori; I didn't want to give her body any bumpier a ride than need be. It's not like I thought she was still in it or anything. It was a matter of respect. And besides, it seemed like all of her I had left.

I felt tired and empty, and kind of half conscious, as if my mind was turned off, but every now and then I'd come out of it and look around. After a while it started to get dark, so I stopped and called to Blue Wing, and asked if he'd like to ride on the folding roof. I suspected he wouldn't, on something moving like that, but he didn't much like flying after dark, either, and it seemed as if he wanted to go with me. Or with Melody, actually; him and her had gotten to be such good friends that fall and winter. Anyway he didn't say a thing, just flew up there and perched, and on we went.

After another couple hours, I stopped and put a feedbag of oats on Socks's nose, and when I got back on the seat, Blue Wing was perched on the arm rest on the rider's side, claustrophobia be darned. I didn't say anything when I sat down, but after we started off again, I reached over and stroked his head a couple of times. "Thanks, old friend," I said, and started crying again. After a while he spoke. I don't think he had the equipment to talk really quietly, but he kept it halfway soft.

"That's not her back there, you know."

"I know," I answered. "But I've got to treat her body with

respect. She lived in it for more than twenty years, and loved me with it, and I loved her with it."

"Do you feel her now?" he asked.

I shook my head. "No. Do you?"

"Yes." He paused half a minute, then went on. "She tells me you will too, when you go to sleep tonight."

He meant it, I didn't doubt. I didn't know whether she'd really talked to him, or if he only imagined it, but he believed what he told me. "How does she seem?" I asked him.

"Different and the same. She is herself, beyond doubt, but without appurtenances or impurities, irritations or anxieties."

"Umm." I looked at that. "I never knew Melody to have anxieties."

"Oh yes. Some of her impatience grew out of anxiety. Anxiety she'd miss something, that it might get away. Everyone, man or raven, has a main inner impediment in life. Impatience was hers."

I thought about that. She'd been patient enough waiting for me, but overall it seemed like he was right. I wondered what my main impediment was. "Is she happy?" I asked.

"Yes she is. If you concentrate, perhaps you can sense her, even awake."

I tried it: made a picture of her in front of me, hoping she might sort of step into it, but she didn't, so I gave up on it and just drove along. After a while I got sleepy, and about half dozed. Then it seemed like there was a light floating above Socks, a sort of round glow maybe three feet across, and I stared at it, not hard, just looking. It was a spirit aura without any body, I realized, and told myself whose it had to be. Although a lot of the pattern was missing.

«Of course, darling,» she thought to me. My hair stood right on end; even the follicles without hair drew up in little cones. «A lot of an aura,» she went on, «goes with living or comes from living.» I started to shake, not scared, but just...*It's really you,* I thought to her, and realized that along with the goose bumps, and the tears running down my face, I was grinning like a fool.

We rode along like that awhile without anything more being

said. There was just a feeling of clear pure love. I don't know how long this went on—fifteen minutes, or an hour or longer. Probably longer, the way things turned out. Then the buggy hit a good bump and my eyes popped open, and the aura was gone. All that was left was a goodbye and a thought—that she loved me, and she'd drop in on me from time to time in my dreams.

I looked to see what Blue Wing had made of all this, or if he even knew, but he was perched there with his head tucked under his wing. So far as I could see, it had all gone by him, and I wondered if maybe I'd been dreaming.

Well, you big lunk, I told myself, *you'll just have to be your own witness. Whatever it was you saw, it seems to have healed your soul. Let it go at that.* Then the goose bumps came back over me, not fierce like before, but in a sort of comfortable wash, and I almost grinned my face in two. *Thank you, Melody,* I thought after her. The feeling kept on fizzing another minute, like soda water, then faded and was gone.

Another half hour or so and I could see the fringe of Teklapori ahead, a darker darkness in the night. I'd been longer on the road than I'd had any idea of.

Chapter 42: Farewell to Tekalos

Melody was gone, but I still needed to burn her body. It's the way things are done in Yuulith. Lots of people there believe ashing the body releases the soul from it; otherwise it has to stay till the body decays. Which may be how it is, if you believe it strongly enough. I could have done it on the farm, but her best friends, along with me and Blue Wing, were Jeremid and Loro. They'd want to be there when the pyre was lit, to say a proper goodbye, and plenty of others would too. And she'd come to the ceremony, for their sake and mine, I had no doubt.

I'm getting ahead of myself though. When I drove up to the barbican, it was late enough that in Six-Month it would have been near dawn, but in Two-Month there was a lot of night left. In spite of my warm cap and coat and mitts, I felt about half froze. Overhead in the gate tower they didn't believe who it was; told me to go away and come back at sunup. I told them somebody better get down there and at least shine a lantern on me, or I'd have their ass on a stick. It took a minute, but finally someone shined a target lantern between the bars of a view slot, and in another half minute what they call "the spy's gate" opened and a guard stepped out. The spy's gate is just wide enough for a man. It's like a ten-foot-long tunnel through the wall. In case of siege, you can use it to let spies in and out after dark. It has a small portcullis at the inner end that they can drop and trap you inside, if they want to. I told the guard who'd opened it I needed to take the gig in. He could see who I was then, and explained apologetically they weren't allowed to open the main gate for anyone after midnight, not even a general. Said it had been the rule for a long long time, peace or war.

That not only irritated me, it felt like an insult to Melody, so I grabbed him by the greatcoat, shook him, and held him up against the stone wall.

"You go back inside," I hissed, "and find the officer of the guard, and tell that son of a bitch General Macurdy will personally flog him right down to the bare ribs if he doesn't get his ass out here right away." And at the time I meant it, though I'd never have done it.

When I let him go, he hurried back inside leaving a string of yessirs behind, and closed the spy's gate after him. It took a few minutes for the officer of the guard to get there—he'd pulled his breeches on over his night shirt and smelled like stale beer—and after seeing for sure who it was, ordered the main gate opened, looking almost as worried about that as he was scared of me. I heard the windlass and chain grind, and watched it raise up. Then I drove the buggy through, and heard it being let down again.

The guards outside the palace itself were no problem. They invited me to sleep in the guard room, but I told them I wouldn't leave Melody. Said I wanted firewood brought out to the graveled walk, and half a dozen blankets. They'd have gotten in trouble if they'd woke up any household help, so while one of them led Socks around to the palace stable, two others brought out wood and kindling, and another came out half buried with army blankets. I laid a fire, lit it with a pass of my hand, wrapped myself in blankets with my feet toward the flames, and went to sleep on the ground.

* * *

I woke up stiff, with frost on my eyebrows. The sun had just come up and was shining in my face. The door guards had kept the fire fed, and when the household help was up and about, they'd told them where I was, and why. So almost as quick as I stood up, the steward came out and asked what I wanted done with "Colonel Melody's mortal remains," volunteering a small building used for holding bodies. Somehow I didn't want to leave it though, and asked him just to let the king and queen know.

And to have something brought out Blue Wing and I could eat. Blue Wing was awake ahead of me, and sat on the roof of the buggy with his feathers fluffed out against the cold.

The food arrived a few minutes ahead of Wollerda. When he came out, it occurred to me that I looked pretty strange—a little crazy, you get right down to it—sitting in the buggy wrapped in blankets, sharing heated-up leftovers of last night's supper roast with a great raven the size of a turkey buzzard. With the frozen body of my wife on the back seat, and the remains of my fire black and gray on his front walk. So when he urged me to come in—the guards would watch the gig, he said—I went inside with him.

Minutes later he was giving orders for a big ceremonial pyre to be built on the parade ground in eight days. That gave him time to have people sent for—officers from the march north, and especially the rebel army—and time for them to get there. I asked what if the weather turned warm, but Liiset said not to worry. Which brought to mind Kittul Kenderson putting a spell on the dead dwarves so they wouldn't spoil. The weather had been a lot warmer then.

* * *

I borrowed a saddle horse and rode north myself to tell Jeremid. It didn't seem right to send someone else. I got there in time for supper, and right away he sent a rider to let Loro know, and Jesper and Tarlok. After we'd eaten, he poured himself wine, while I drank sassafras.

"I don't know what to say, Macurdy," he told me. "I expected you two to grow old together. I'd decided early on the best I could hope for was, she might marry me if you got your Varia back. But as long as she had a chance with you, she'd never settle for anyone else."

Grow old together. That was one thing we couldn't have done, unless Varia'd pulled off a miracle with her; I'd figured that when the time came, she'd get old and I'd take care of her. Old age wouldn't have been a problem, I didn't think, though it might have been tough for a while when she found out she was aging and I wasn't.

Jeremid hadn't gotten married. Instead, he had himself three concubines. For different moods, he said. I don't think I could be happy that way, but his aura told me he was. Content, anyway.

I hadn't planned to spend the night there, but I did. When it got late, he offered me the company of one of his concubines for the night. I told him I wasn't ready for something like that yet.

* * *

The day of the fire was mild and bright and still. There were probably a couple thousand veterans of the invasion, a lot of them exrebels down from the hills, plus palace staff and thousands of townfolk. The pyre was a big one, and it was me who lit it off, of course. It took off quick—a small fortune in lamp oil had been poured on it—and the smoke rose straight up. Folks stood there till the whole pile burnt down; took a while. It's sort of a rule you don't walk off early from a funeral fire. And way up high—about as high as birds fly, I guess—I could see Blue Wing soaring in big circles.

* * *

That evening I ate with Wollerda and Liiset and Jeremid. And Omara. Liiset had invited her; she'd been assigned as Liiset's secretary, lady-in-waiting, and healer to the palace.

Wollerda asked me again to go to Duinarog as his ambassador, but I told him no. There'd likely be too many ylver who'd resent me, the general of the invasion that killed so many of them. And anyway I didn't want to. Then Liiset asked if I'd reconsider going to the Cloister. She believed Sarkia was having second thoughts about a lot of things in her life. There wasn't any question now: she was in decline after more than two hundred years. I told Liiset I appreciated the invite, but I just wasn't willing. That she should send Sarkia my thanks, and my best wishes that she could wrap things up all right.

Next she said I'd need someone to look after household matters for me on the farm. And if I wanted, Omara was willing to take the job.

For just a minute I was tempted. I already had plans of my own I hadn't let on, and they included getting further trained in healing. She'd be as good a teacher as I could hope to have, and I liked Omara, liked how serious and honest she was. And for looks, she was scarcely behind Varia and Liiset. But I said no to that too. Making sure Omara knew I liked and admired her.

That's when I told them I wasn't going to stay in Tekalos.

"Where are you going?" Wollerda asked surprised.

"Back home to Farside," I told him.

You could have heard a pin drop.

"When?"

"I'm leaving here tomorrow. By way of the farm, to tell the staff I'm going, and to get Hog. They'll take care of things till you sell the place to someone."

He sat there stunned, so I explained. "An awful lot has happened to me: I started a war where thousands of men died. And loved two women and lost them both. Now I need to get away, let things settle out in my mind. I can help my dad on the farm, probably log some, and just be in my own world awhile. Then… then I expect I'll come back. I'm not sure why, but it seems to me I will."

I didn't say anything about what I planned to do before I crossed over.

* * *

After we'd done talking, Wollerda invited me to his bath. Not Jeremid and me, just me. But when I got there, Liiset was there too. Standing nekkit like that, she'd have quickened a statue, so I got right in the water before I got a hardon. We talked a bit, and Wollerda asked me to stay for just a few months—long enough to help him with some problems. We talked about them awhile, and I got some ideas I told him about, but I could see he really didn't need me. He just figured if I stayed around that long, I'd be over losing Melody and decide not to go.

Liiset told me going through the other way was a lot different than coming through to Yuulith. She made it sound kind of like a hole opening in a water tank, squirting water through in one direction. Anyone could go through with the flow, the problem being whether you arrived alive or dead, sane or insane. But going through the other way, against the pressure so to speak, seemed to be possible only if you had enough ylvin blood and talent.

I didn't worry about it. I had no doubt I could do it. Anyway, after a few minutes, I said I needed to get some sleep, which was true enough, so we got out and dried off, and I left.

In my room, I'd just gone to bed when someone rapped on the door. I figured it was Jeremid, curious about what got said in the hot tub, so I called out, "Just a minute," and going over, turned the latch and opened it.

It was Omara standing there.

"Hi," I said. "What brings you here?" I was pretty sure I knew.

"Liiset suggested I come."

"Suggested? Or ordered?"

"Suggested. She is not Sarkia or Idri."

Her aura showed no sign of lying. I could feel old junior swelling, and found myself stepping back, letting her in. I watched my hand close the door behind her, turn the latch and set the bolt.

"I was glad to," she went on. "Wanted to. You are a very attractive man, Macurdy. Compelling." She stepped out of her robe then, nekkit as could be, and twice as pretty.

"Well then," I said, and peeled off my nightshirt. We put our arms around each other and kissed, then kissed some more, warm and wet. She felt good, awfully good, pressed up against me. After a minute we went to bed, and I drew the bed curtains.

After a while we got up and washed. "You are a very nice lover, Macurdy," she said. "But why did you draw the curtains?"

That kind of surprised me. "To keep the warmth in," I told her.

"I thought so. Are you unable to keep yourself warm with the mind?"

"Warm with the mind?"

According to her it was simple enough; most folks with much talent could learn. "It's limited, unfortunately," she went on. "It simply increases the rate at which the body creates heat from the food you eat, and circulates that heat. You can even concentrate it into your fingers and toes. It doesn't suffice for severe weather, though. Had you been unclothed and outside in the bitter weather recently, you'd soon have felt cold, and after a time would have frozen." She looked at me as if considering something. "There is another, very superior technique requiring more talent, but it takes careful training. As in fire starting, you do it by drawing heat from the Web of the World. The difficulty lies in control; you can easily and quickly injure or kill yourself with it. I can train you to use it safely, if you'd like."

"How long would it take?"

"Two or three days, perhaps. Or a week."

My glands were telling me, "Say yes, Macurdy, you fool," but I heard my mouth saying: "Omara, that's something I'd like to learn, and you're the one I'd like to learn it from, but—" I shrugged. "I want to go home to Farside. It feels to me like it's what I need to do, what I'm supposed to do. And if I don't go now, I may not ever."

"I understand," she said, and I think she really did.

She stayed awhile, to teach me the technique for warming the body from inside, and for me there wasn't any trick to that one at all. Then we got friendly again, and after that she put her robe back on and left.

Just for the heck of it, I left my nightshirt off and slept on top the covers that night, warm as toast. The only thing was, at breakfast next morning, with Wollerda and Liiset, I ate about twice as much as usual.

Chapter 43: Vulkan

After breakfast I said goodbye to folks. A little bit dishonestly, letting them think I'd be going from the farm to Ferny Cove, in case Sarkia got ideas. Then I drove Socks and the buggy back to the farm, where I packed stuff to take with me—not very much—and went over things with the foreman and steward. I spent the night in our old bedroom; had a little spate of grief, but it passed. Then, early the next morning, rode north on Hog to the Valley Highway and headed west, taking neither remount nor pack horse. Just some silver so I could sleep at inns, and some gold coins about the size of double eagles to use on Farside, and to pay Arbel for the training I wanted. Being alone, and not caring to sit around a potroom in the evening, I generally rode late. If I didn't come to an inn, I slept in a barn. I didn't trouble to count the days.

* * *

The house looked like it had when I'd left Wolf Springs. Lamplight shone through the cracks between the shutters, and thin smoke rose from three of the chimneys, flattening out above the roof in a layer that by moonlight looked like cotton gauze. Getting down off Hog, I knocked at the door.

It was Hauser that opened it. He stood there for a minute with his mouth open, then grinned, stepped outside, and shook my hand. For a minute I thought he was going to hug me! "Macurdy!" he said. "What brings you here? I've been picturing you in a manor somewhere, or a palace! Come in!"

"I'll stable my horse first," I said. He said he'd do it, but I said I'd better, Hog being touchy with strangers. In the horse shed, I lit the lamp with my finger, hung up Hog's tack, and curried him three-four minutes, which was plenty, given the winter weather. Then I went back to the house.

I'd hardly knocked again before Hauser opened the door. Arbel was standing with him, and gave me one of his long looks. Then he grinned bigger than I'd ever seen him before; grins aren't Arbel's specialty. "So," he said, "the hero of Wolf Springs returns. It's good to see you, Macurdy." He led us to his parlor and we all three sat down. "What brings you back?"

He'd called me the hero of Wolf Springs! And his aura said he was being sarcastic! "I'm going back to Farside," I told him, "and Oz wasn't a whole lot farther than Ferny Cove. Besides, I was in Oztown twice, getting ready for the war, and never got to Wolf Springs to apologize or thank you. You did a lot for me, and I've always felt bad about leaving Oz the way I did. It must have hurt your reputation. Wolf Springs' too."

Arbel laughed. "Hurt my reputation? You became famous in Oz as the man who climbed a tree to drive a jaguar out. The man who beat up half the House of Heroes, or at least a number of them, including a sergeant famous as a brawler, and rode off with the best looking, most daring and admired spear maiden in Oz. And then became really famous for the war."

My jaw must have been down on my chest when he finished, but it didn't stay there long, because the next thing he said was, "Where is your spear maiden?"

I didn't tell him flat out; I led into it. "She and I were leaders in the rebellion that got Pavo crowned king," I said, "and she was with me all the way through the war. She was a colonel, wounded at the Battle of Ternass. Then we got married. She died about three weeks ago. Drowned." I told him how it happened, how Blue Wing had fetched me—the whole thing except how terrible I'd felt. "We burned her body outside the palace," I finished. "The king and queen were there, and a couple thousand veterans of the war. Not to mention most of Teklapori. She was well-known and much admired."

Arbel shook his head, looking sober. "A grievous loss, Macurdy," he said. "I can see the scar. I can also see you've healed." None of us said anything more right away. Then he smiled a little. "You've gotten a reputation as a wizard, too. You killed the evil Quaie with a ball of fire…"

My eyes must have bugged out. "How did you hear about that?" I asked.

"The story spread through the empire and Marches; merchants carried it from there. It reached Oz this winter. And our troops brought home other stories. Perhaps exaggerated."

"Probably." It was an invitation to tell him stories, and I would before I left, but not just then. "You asked what brought me here. I told you part of it, but there's more." I stopped then. I'd been taking it for granted he'd say yes. "If you'll change your mind," I went on, "and teach me more of the shaman's profession, mainly the healing skills, I'd like to try them on Farside. I'll be glad to pay you for your trouble."

He laughed out loud. "But you're not sure I will, because I sent you to the militia. Well. I'll be happy to. But first, tell me what magicks you've demonstrated since I saw you last."

I did, not leaving out about my new teeth, though I could hardly take credit for them. It'd been Varia's spells, and from there, my jaws had taken over. I told him the luck I'd had with the healing he'd taught me, him and Omara, and about learning to keep myself warm. And about looking into the eye holes in that skull on the headwaters of the Tuliptree; to me that was bigger magic than the way I'd killed Quaie. "I guess when I was here before," I said, "I wasn't really ready to learn much."

Arbel laughed, then we sat around and talked about different things. He'd found an apprentice he liked—a twelve-year-old girl with a lot of talent, who went home before supper. That was the disadvantage of having a young girl as an apprentice, he said; you couldn't very well keep them around in the evening. Folks might get the wrong idea.

Ozians are pretty free and easy, but they don't put up with a man humping children. The punishment is, they tie you up, set you astraddle of a log, nail your cod to it, stack wood around you, and put a dull knife in your free hand. Then they light the wood. If you saw off your cod, you're a castrate, and a slave into the bargain. If you don't, you won't suffer very long, but it might seem like it.

Hauser wasn't talking, just listening, and anyway, his face, and the way he sat, and his aura all told me he was looking in, not out. It came to me that what I'd said about going back to Farside must have hit him hard. I could go because I had ylvin blood, and talent, and some training, while he didn't and couldn't.

While I was at it, I told them about other magicks I'd seen, like Kittul Kendersson "blessing" my sword, and weaving a spell so the dead dwarves wouldn't swell and stink. And about the Sisters that went with the army to heal wounds, and Quaie's shock fingers he'd used on me.

I also told him what Omara said about keeping warm by drawing heat from what she called the "Web of the World," and the dangers in learning it. That really got Arbel's interest. He said he was going to try working it out for himself.

He also told me magic misused, even accidentally, kicked back on the magician sooner or later, and big magic was at least as dangerous to the user as to anyone else. There'd been folks who'd set out to develop really big powers, but they died in the process.

After a while it got late, and Arbel put me up in a small guest room with a clean straw sack on the bed. I stripped, put on my nightshirt and lay down, wishing Omara would come through the door like she had at the palace. How I felt about her wasn't anything like I'd felt about Varia or Melody, but I liked her a lot. She was a good person, and just then I was lonesome, in spite of being in the same house with two old friends, and another probably perched on the roof beside a chimney.

I thought about Hauser, too. I could stay in Yuulith and be a big shot if I wanted, in Tekalos or at the Cloister, and probably in Oz or other places. Or be Wollerda's ambassador at Duinarog. But instead I was going back to Farside, to the farm. While Hauser could probably be a professor on Farside, but in Oz he was a slave. Couldn't go back, even if they'd let him.

Then I got thinking about the dangers Arbel had mentioned in big powerful magicks, and told myself I better be careful with fireballs. Sarkia was supposed to have practiced magic for two hundred years and stayed young and healthy. And was only now declining; something I wouldn't mention to Arbel. But from what I'd heard about Ferny Cove, from some Kormehri and from Sarkia herself, she hadn't used magicks for weapons, only for protection—confusion spells, invisibility spells, spells to raise fogs and mists. And tracking magic. Things like that. Maybe magicks like those didn't kick back on a person.

What with all the thoughts running through my head, I must have laid there an hour before I got to sleep.

* * *

The next day my lessons started. Like before, Arbel said I should do other stuff too, to keep grounded, and offered to get a slave girl sent in for me once a week, like he did for himself. I was tempted, but instead, for a few mornings, I saddled up Hog and rode around the countryside a couple hours. Then I took a notion to train with Isherhohm's militia veterans on Six-Day afternoons, for the exercise and to keep my hand in. They'd nearly all of them been in the war, and I'd been the commander, but Isherhohm treated me like just another veteran.

The morning after the first workout, I was sore all over, really sore! I'd gone soft! Never thought that could happen to me. So I started taking an ax and trotting out to the woods in the morning, where I'd cut logs and firewood for a couple hours.

I'd figured Blue Wing had come along mainly to see someone go through a gate, but he told me it was because Melody and I had gotten to be his best friends, and now she was gone, and pretty soon I'd be. Whatever. In Oz he didn't hang around close all that much, any more than he had on the farm. He even flew west once to visit Maikel. Anyway I set it up with the local butcher to keep him supplied with cutting scraps that otherwise would have gone to the hogs or the dogs. Most of our talking got done in the woods, where he'd drop in on me pretty often. But he'd be gone days at a time.

Cutting wood, I'd take a few minutes every day to practice throwing the ax at a tree. And the knife Arbel gave me when I went off to the Heroes. Stuck them better than ever, which made me wonder if magic played any part in it.

Whatever. Trotting and chopping every day made me feel

good; toughened me and gave me more energy. And the lessons went really well, a lot better and faster than when Arbel had tried teaching me before. My very first day back, he'd said I was already better than lots of shamans—a late starter but fast learner. Kerin, his real apprentice, was bright and sharp, and already getting tall, but kid-skinny. And dark, with big, bright, dark eyes, a sharp curved nose like an Aye-rab, and a little narrow mouth. Lots of times he'd just give her something to do and leave her to do it, while he worked with me. I felt a little awkward about that, but he said he had years to work with her, while I wanted to be on my way. No later than Four-Month, I'd told him. Part of what he had Kerin doing was preparing dried herbs for him; and practicing to read and write, which lots of Ozians could barely do; and practicing ceremonial magic that could be used to bring rain or cancel curses—things like that. I didn't figure to learn either one; I didn't much believe in curses or rain spells. Arbel didn't seem to make much of them either, but if Ozians did, I suppose he had to go through the motions.

He took a different approach with me than before. I'd told him how Varia had taught me meditation, which she'd set me up for early on by spelling me. So he tried teaching me stuff when I was in a meditation trance, and liked how it worked. Better than just spelling me, he said, because under a spell you're less doing than being done to, while in a meditation trance you did it yourself. A matter of self-responsibility, he said.

Right from the start I did a fair job of healing injuries. Arbel was famous for his healing, and folks came or got brought to him from miles around. One guy he worked with me on had split his foot with an ax, and another'd got slashed in a knife fight, and a little girl had fallen in her ma's cook fire. Mostly what he did was refine, and strengthen quite a bit, what I could already do for wounds like those. Taught me to focus better.

Except for the little girl that fell in the fire: I didn't know anything about healing burns; all I could have done was use a sort of general spell that would give relief from the pain, and speed the healing some. He showed me things just for burns.

Where I was weakest was in healing the sick. He had different spells for different sicknesses. Some sickness, he told me, comes from the mind. Asthma was sort of like that. Some folks could get asthma from their mind alone. Others were allergic to something—hay more often than not—but get them away from the hay, they'd keep the asthma for hours or days, or even longer, because of something in their mind that held it there. It could even kill them. When someone got asthma from hay, they could come to him and he'd treat the mind, and the asthma would quit right away, instead of hanging on. After that they could still get asthma from hay, but usually, take them away from the hay, and the asthma was gone in minutes. Commonly rashes disappeared in minutes too, at least the itching eased, and the rash would almost always be gone within the day. Rheumatism might go just as quick, or take a few days, or it could hang on.

He even showed me how to make tumors shrink up and disappear. That didn't always work either, but sometimes it did, and sometimes the tumor didn't come back. And when someone got brought in that had what I'd call pneumonia, he couldn't make it go away right off, but usually they'd feel better right away, and well, after a night's sleep. They'd be back working in two or three days, instead of a couple weeks.

Like anything else, what he did had its limits. Sometimes someone wasn't helped at all—everyone dies sooner or later—and he said the shaman who couldn't live with that had better quit and go to farming, for peace of mind. For me, not being perfect wouldn't be any problem; I'd been doing it all my life.

* * *

It was a mild sunny morning in Three-Month when I met Vulkan. Or when Vulkan found me. I'd felled a tree and was chopping logs out of it when I heard Blue Wing yelling from way up high, I couldn't tell what. Then I felt someone looking at me—someone of *power*—and turned around. And almost shit myself! There was a BIG boar hog standing between two trees watching me. Not that he looked like any hog I'd ever seen, not even a razorback. I could tell he was a hog, but for size he reminded me more of a shorthorn bull, a good four feet high at his humped shoulders. He had a thick coat of bristly hair, dark gray on the sides and nearly black along the back. His tusks looked like ivory sickle blades, and I'd judge his weight at better than half a ton. There was no doubt at all that were he to meet a bear in the woods, that bear would go up a tree quick as a wink, crying for its mama.

I should have been scared to death, but after the first shock I wasn't; somehow I knew he wasn't there to rip me up. So I stepped onto the log I'd just cut, squatted there and looked at him.

«So you are the one.»

His "voice" was deep and hollow, like someone talking with an empty milk pail over his head, but somehow I knew there wasn't really any sound to it—that the words had come into my head without him ever speaking. "Could be," I said. "It depends on who the one's supposed to be." That amused him; I could feel it. "Sounds as if you're looking for someone in particular," I went on. "What brings you?"

«An urge. The purpose will no doubt unfold itself for us in good time.» His hooves, the only dainty thing about him, brought him a few steps closer. «Your aura marks you as someone of power,» he said. «A ruler and magician.»

He had an aura too, all animals do, but with all that hog to look at, I'd paid it no attention. Now I did. It wasn't what I think of as an animal aura. More like yours or mine or Blue Wing's, but different. His spirit aura showed at least as much power as that giant body. I wondered if all great boars were like him, and he answered my question without my putting it into words.

«We are alike, they and I, in being magicians, and in essence, rulers. And in various other respects. But still we vary one from the other, though less than humans do.»

Then he just stood there. It seemed like if he'd come looking for me, it was up to him to lead the conversation. But if he didn't know why he'd come, maybe I ought to keep things going till he remembered or figured it out, or decided to leave. "My name's Macurdy," I told him. "What's yours?"

He didn't answer for a minute. Then, «You may call me Vulkan,» he said. «We do not have names, but I like that one.»

After another half minute with neither of us saying anything, I tried something else. ">From what I've heard, you folks eat animals, and I've seen where one of you rooted up skunk-cabbage and ate it. But big as you are, it must take a lot to keep you fed. Seems like you'd leave more sign around than you do."

«We are quite rare, and at any rate do not eat a great deal; we draw our energy from the Web of the World, as you think of it. But as yours do, our bodies require certain substances, minerals for example, though not in large quantities. Thus we must eat, but not nearly in proportion to our size.

«And now I begin to see—begin to—why I was drawn to speak with you. You are from Farside, and...Ah yes, Macurdy! Of course. And you plan to leave Yuulith, to return whence you came.»

How could he have known that? Unless he read it in my mind. Or was I imagining things? No, he was there all right. I'd seen enough else strange in Yuulith that I wasn't going to doubt my eyes. And Blue Wing must have seen him; that must have been what got him all excited. It seemed like if any of this was imaginary, it was his "talking" to me. So far he hadn't moved, except early when he'd come a few steps closer, and to flick his little fly-whisk tail a few times. Hadn't even moved his mouth. But his aura and eyes told of power way beyond anything the Sisters had shown me.

I decided to ask him questions—see what he'd say. "I've heard that all of you are boars," I said, "that there aren't any sows of your kind. Is that true?"

«Boars? Let us simply say you heard correctly: there are no sows.»

"Well then, uh, who births you?"

«We are not born in the usual sense. We come from the inbetween, one might say. Inaccurately, of course.»

I didn't know what to make of that. "How could you come to be, without a sow to birth you?"

He chuckled again inside my head. «The All-Spirit provides us with bodies. There is no sexuality among us.»

"But then—" He seemed to be saying they got born without

any breeding taking place, or any sow giving birth. I let that be. Instead I asked him: "How did you get to Yuulith from the inbetween?" Whatever that was.

«We do not use gates. We once were humans, and enter Yuulith in the spirit, from the place of rest and recovery. We receive our bodies here. We are old souls, who have lived out the normal prerequisites for permanent retirement from the choices and lessons of life. And should have graduated, you might say. But instead have been sent here as volunteers, to prepare ourselves for some purpose we will remember, or discover, when it is time.»

I had no idea at all what to ask next. I just looked at him, maybe eleven, twelve hundred pounds of bone, muscle, and tusks, roaming around the back country rooting up skunk-cabbage and eating wild game, and maybe from time to time somebody's calf. All to prepare himself for he didn't know what.

«And you are returning to Farside,» he said. «Well. In time, if you live, you will return here. I will find you then, for I sense we have things to do together.»

I just stared.

«And now I will grant you a favor. As a sign.»

"A favor?"

«Tomorrow you will know the favor you want. It will be foremost in your mind when you waken. When you know, I will know, even at a distance. And whatever it is, it will be yours.»

Then, without another word, he turned and trotted off.

* * *

I never did go home for my day's lesson from Arbel. Instead I sheathed my ax and hiked around in the woods, a thousand thoughts running through my head, not to mention the questions Blue Wing asked. He'd lit in a tree to watch and listen, but hadn't heard any of what Vulkan thought to me, though he'd heard me talking to Vulkan, of course.

Part of what I thought about was what favor I'd get. Could Vulkan give me Melody back? Or Varia, with her and Cyncaidh's blessing? What would be on my mind when I woke up in the morning? Could he really do it?

Along toward evening my mind settled out, and I headed back for Arbel's. I told him about meeting Vulkan, and he was impressed, but I didn't mention the promised favor. Didn't feel ready to. Besides, having spent most of the day hiking in the woods, talking in a warm room made me drowsy. I excused myself, went to bed, and fell straight to sleep, like a stone.

Chapter 44: Farewell to Yuulith

The next morning I woke up with something on my mind all right: I wanted to take Hauser back to Missouri with me. Apparently that was to be my favor. Not to have Melody back, like I'd half expected; maybe because there were limits to what was possible. Or Varia, probably because it would be against her will. But Hauser. Which to my mind meant it was somehow possible to take him through. And now I'd have to tell Arbel, which I didn't look forward to. Hauser had been his slave—actually the village's, but his to use—for quite a few years.

As soon as I got dressed, I went and told Arbel what I wanted to do. He looked me over half smiling, his aura showing no sign of upset. "Why do you think I'd object?" he asked. He could read me like a book.

"I thought you might not want to let him go. He's given you some good ideas, and he's a good worker—and better company than most."

Arbel grunted. "You're right; maybe I should object." He smiled then. "In his self-chosen function as an artisan here, he has given me far more than routine service. It would be shameful to begrudge him his return."

He cocked an eyebrow. "You realize, of course, that I do not own him. He's property of the village. But if I'm willing to give up his services, the council will approve. They might, even if I weren't; you're a much bigger hero here than you recognize. But the real issue is, how will you get him through? Do you have a magic you haven't told me about?"

His sharp eyes were watching my aura, I had no doubt, and

I couldn't see any way around it but to tell him about Vulkan's favor, so I did. "And I take that to mean he can," I finished.

For a minute, Arbel just stared, then he turned thoughtful. "Assume he can. Assume your Vulkan has such power. Is there any guarantee Hauser will arrive sane? Or even alive?"

I hadn't given that a thought. "Vulkan didn't seem like someone who'd send him through a gate to arrive dead or crazy."

Arbel shrugged. "Perhaps not, if he understood the problem. I have no experience with anyone coming out in Farside."

"I'm trusting Vulkan's honesty and judgment," I said. "And his power to make it happen right."

Arbel nodded. "Let's ask Hauser," he said.

I hadn't thought of that. "I guess we'd better. But let's not mention Vulkan."

We went into the kitchen, where Hauser was restocking the wood pile. "Charles," I said softly, "if you could go back to Farside, would you? Even if it was dangerous?"

He stared at me for a long five or ten seconds, while it soaked through I was serious. Then he turned white and started to shake, leaning against the wall to keep from falling down. I could honest to God feel his feelings. Nobody said anything for half a minute; then I told him I thought maybe I could get him through. "Arbel says it's fine with him, and he thinks the council will allow it. Do you want to try?"

He nodded dumbly at me.

"Well then," I said, and turned to Arbel. "Will you ask the council?"

* * *

Arbel asked the village headman that same day. The council met next evening, and what all might have been said, I didn't hear, but the decision was Hauser could go if the gate would take him. I went around to each councilman the day after that and thanked him. None of them seemed to think it was any big deal as long as Arbel was happy with it.

I felt pretty sure Vulkan's magic could get him through okay, but I wanted to prepare him as much as I could. Like most people's, Hauser's aura showed some talent, more than most, but nothing like an ylf, for example.

I put myself in a meditation trance and had Arbel ask me to remember everything Varia'd done when she spelled me the first two times. The drills I could remember without any trance.

Working with Hauser was good training for me. The first time I felt a little spooked to do it, and afterward I wasn't sure we'd accomplished anything. I did the first spell, and the instructions and questions that went with it, three nights in a row. Then, with him in a shallow spell again, I taught him to meditate. That seemed to pick it up. On later evenings I drilled him, and we could see him start changing.

My own training kept going along fast, even though I was giving time and attention to Hauser. Not only my training in healing, but other training I hadn't figured to do. I still aimed to leave during Four-Month, on the noon nearest the full moon, which on their calendar is always just before the middle of the month.

I felt more than ready, and Hauser seemed to have gone as far as he could. He'd even learned to keep himself warm from inside, and to start fire—way more than we'd ever expected of him. Arbel, though, figured getting through was more a question of inborn talent than how far you'd taken it. Unless of course Vulkan did it for him. Me, I had faith in Vulkan's magic; the training was just to help Hauser survive.

Something else happened that last week, too. Unknown to me, Arbel had been experimenting on keeping the body warm by tapping into the Web of the World, and had worked out a procedure that seemed safe, if done right. Anyway it worked for him. He told me about it on my last day, and wrote out all the steps. There wasn't time to practice them under his supervision, but if I was careful, I could practice them alone on Farside. I gave them a quick look-over; they didn't seem all that hard.

That was the evening before the gate was due to open. It was also the evening I told Hauser about Vulkan and what he'd promised, and that all the work we'd done was just in case. I'd wanted him to think it was all up to him. Now he was ready as he could get, and I wanted to ease his nerves.

* * *

Before I went to bed that night, I sat in front of the fire thinking about what might have been. About Melody. She'd died being what she'd always been: impetuous, reckless. She'd loved me strongly, and I'd loved her, but she was what she was; that's how the world worked. And about Varia. It still seemed as if I'd come back to Yuulith someday, and it came to me that she and I weren't done with one another yet. I shook it off. She was married to a high ylf lord, and they were happy together; had a kid, and they'd probably have more. As far as that's concerned, he was probably a better husband for her anyway, really.

I thought about Omara, too: If I'd stayed, I could have been happy with her. There mightn't ever have been any powerful love between us, but we'd have made up for that with respect and consideration, and good times in bed. But somehow, as much sense as it made, it wasn't right for me. I needed to go back to Farside.

I ended up meditating a little to still my mind. Worked like a charm. When I lay down, I went right to sleep.

* * *

And woke up fresh and confident. Had breakfast and went for a ride on Hog. I'd miss Hog; we'd been through a lot together. He'd be Arbel's now.

When Arbel's sundial said it was time, Arbel went with us. So did Blue Wing. I'd thought about what I'd say if Blue Wing wanted to go through the gate with me. Not that I thought he would, but just in case. Even if it would take him, if crossing to Farside was anything like crossing to Yuulith, he'd arrive without a feather left. And if he got there okay, some sonofabitch would likely shoot him and get him stuffed.

But he never asked, just flew along sober as a judge. After two mild rainy days, the field of buckwheat we walked through was growing strong and thick, and green as you please. The sun was out, and the day as warm as any since the fall before. I could see by Hauser's aura he was confident, even though the dark circles under his eyes told me he hadn't slept much. He could have—he knew how to still his mind now. Maybe he'd wanted to spend the night thinking and remembering, or maybe planning. As for me—I'd wait and see how things looked when I got there, likely help Dad for a while, then maybe go wandering. See more of my own world.

In the grove, the basswood buds were opening and the dogwoods were in bloom. It wasn't noon yet; we'd left early enough not to be late. I looked at Hauser and he looked at me. He was sort of grinning, but not saying anything.

We didn't any of us know exactly how long it'd be before high noon: about a quarter hour, Arbel thought. Hauser and I each had a small pouch of Teklan silver coins in our pack, and I still had most of the gold coins I'd started out with a couple months earlier. Arbel had only been willing to take one of them for his time and trouble, and I'd given three of them to Hauser.

I felt it quicker'n Arbel, then Blue Wing gave a big squawk. Something was pressing on me, just enough to notice, from off to one side. I grabbed Hauser by an arm, and walked against the pressure, which was getting stronger fast. It wasn't affecting the trees, even the saplings weren't bending from it. I guess it only affected animals.

Arbel called out, "Good luck, Macurdy!" I knew it was him, but his voice sounded strange, tinny. I glanced back, and he looked all crooked and jiggedy. I glimpsed Blue Wing, too; he looked like three or four great ravens half mixed together, flying in a little circle, and his calling had a shrill buzzing sound, reminded me of a musical saw.

I realized Hauser was walking against the pressure as easily as I was, but I held onto his arm anyway. My hair stood on end more than any time in my life before. This was nothing at all like coming through from Farside. A big humming started that somehow I knew was loud, yet I could hardly hear it, and I felt like I was vibrating apart.

Suddenly everything went black as tar; blacker, as if there wasn't such a thing as light. The sound stopped, and the pressure, and the vibrating, but I still felt Hauser's arm in my right hand; I was gripping it harder than I ought to. For just a few seconds it was like that, still and absolutely black, then I felt myself drop a foot or two onto my back, a stone bruising my ribs. There was moonlight, but for half a minute I just lay there, dizzy, my stomach queasy, my eyes not able to focus. Then things steadied out, and I saw some scrawny pine tops against the night sky. Injun Knob. I turned my head and there was Hauser.

It was him that said it, sounding awed. "We're home, Macurdy. We're home."

Books Published by Sky Warrior Books

Purchase them through online resellers and better independent bookstores everywhere. Visit us at www.skywarriorbooks.com **for news, upcoming books, and promotions.**

Alma Alexander

2012: Midnight at Spanish Gardens (E-book, Trade Paperback)

Cybermage (E-book)

Embers of Heaven (E-book, Trade Paperback)

Gift of the Unmage (E-book)

Spellspam (E-book)

S. A. Bolich

Firedancer (E-book, Trade Paperback)

Seaborn (E-book)

Windrider (E-Book, Trade Paperback)

L. J. Bonham

The Debt (E-book)

Shield of Honor (E-book)

Wolves of Valhalla (E-book)

M. H. Bonham

Daemons and Shadows (E-book)

Prophecy of Swords (E-book)

Runestone of Teiwas (E-book)

Samurai Son (E-book, Trade Paperback)

Serpent Singer and Other Stories (E-book)

The Spirit Wolf (E-book)

Robert W. Brady Jr.

Indomitus Est (E-book)

Indomitus Vivat (E-book)

Bob Brown

The Dragon, The Damsel, and the Knight (YA E-book)

The Lost Enforcer (E-book, Trade Paperback)

John Dalmas

The Lion of Farside Volume 1 (E-book, Trade Paperback)

The Lion of Farside Volume 2 (E-book, Trade Paperback)

Signature of God Volume 1(E-book)

Signature of God Volume 2 (E-book)

Soldiers! Part 1(E-book)

Soldiers! Part 2 (E-book)

The General's President (E-book)

The Second Coming (E-book, Trade Paperback)

Deby Fredericks

Seven Exalted Orders (E-book, Trade Paperback)

Carol Hightshoe (Editor)

Zombiefied: An Anthology of All Things Zombie (E-book, Trade Paperback)

Gary Jonas

Acheron Highway (E-book)

Dragon Gate (E-book)

Modern Sorcery (E-book, Trade Paperback)

One-Way Ticket to Midnight (E-book)

Quick Shots (E-book, Trade Paperback)

Frog and Esther Jones

Coup de Grace (E-book, Trade Paperback)

Grace Under Fire (E-book)

Pat MacEwen

The Dragon's Kiss (E-book)

Rough Magic (E-book)

Christie Meierz

The Marann (E-book)

Michael J. Parry

The Oaks Grove (E-book)

The Spiral Tattoo (E-book)

Phyllis Irene Radford

Healing Waves: A Charity Anthology for Japan (Editor) (E-book)

How Beer Saved the World (Editor) (E-book, Trade Paperback)

Gears and Levers 1: A Steampunk Anthology (Editor) (E-book, Trade Paperback)

Gears and Levers 2: A Steampunk Anthology (Editor) (E-book, Trade Paperback)

Gears and Levers 3: A Steampunk Anthology (Editor) (E-book)

Lacing Up for Murder, A Whistling River Mystery (E-book)

The Lost Enforcer (E-book, Trade Paperback)

So You Want to Commit Novel (E-book, Trade Paperback)

Dusty Rainbolt (Editor)

The Mystical Cat (E-book)

Deborah J. Ross (Editor)

The Feathered Edge (E-book, Trade Paperback)

Laura J. Underwood

Ard Magister (Book One of Ard Magister) (E-book)

Ard Magister: Demon in the Bones (Book Two of Ard Magister) (E-book)

Dragon's Tongue (Book One of the Demon-Bound) (E-book)

The Hounds of Ardagh (E-book)

Steven E. Wedel (Editor)

Tails of the Pack (E-book)